The
D·N·A
Detectives

The Smuggler's Daughter

Dr. Mandy Hartley

To my beautiful children, Annabelle and Harry.
My very own "DNA Detectives".

Published by SJH Publishing

298 Regents Park Road, London N3 2SZ

020 8371 4000

sjhpublishing.org

ISBN 978-1-906670-59-7

Cover design and illustrations: Jamie Mckerrow Maxwell

Printed and bound by CPI Group (UK) Ltd, Croydon, CR0 4YY

Foreword

Hopefully you will have read and enjoyed my first book "The DNA Detectives – To Catch a Thief" so you will know that when I was at school I always loved science. I decided to go to university so I could study science in greater depth, in particular the biology of diseases. You will also know that it was when I was at university that something very magical happened; a light-bulb moment that mapped out my future career. It was the moment when I was working in the laboratory and I saw DNA in a tube for the first time. That is when I knew I wanted to work with DNA, a subject that has given me the most incredible career. I have been fortunate to have worked in many different laboratories all over the country, on many different species and in many different fields, including population genetics, inheritance of genetic diseases, establishing family relationships and forensic science. It has been the most incredible journey and now I get to share what I have learnt with children all over the world through my books, stories and workshops.

The idea for this book "The DNA Detectives – The Smuggler's Daughter" has been in my head for a very long time and writing it all down was a big relief! When I was really young we used to go to Cornwall for our holidays. I fell in love with the rugged coastline and the beautiful hidden sandy coves with crystal-clear waters. I was obsessed with the stories about the Cornish ship wreckers and how it is alleged that on stormy nights they would leave out false lights so ships thinking they had found safety were lured to their doom on the rocks. The ship wreckers would then plunder the bounty from the ship and smuggle it ashore. When I was young I loved exploring caves on the beaches, convinced they were home to smugglers' tunnels.

What a pleasure it was to research this book with my mum. We headed to Mullion Cove in Cornwall and stayed in a guest house reported to have a smugglers' tunnel running underneath it to the beach. Unfortunately, to this day the tunnel has never been found. We headed to a beach called Gunwalloe on our trip, where caves were said to be linked by a smugglers' tunnel to the belfry of a nearby church, and another passage joined The Halzephron Inn to Fishing Cove, the home of a local smuggler called Henry Cuttance. It was like being a child again looking for the entrance to the tunnels on the beach. But, of course, we realised they would be well hidden and despite an extensive search we couldn't find them. However, on visiting The Halzephron Inn we saw its timbers, which are made from the many local ship wrecks, and the bar counter, which is hundreds of years old. The staff showed us a really thick wall in the main bar, behind which is a shaft leading down to the cellar that was supposed to have been used by the smugglers. This gave me lots of ideas for the story and my imagination went into overdrive!

Mum and I also visited the famous Jamaica Inn on Bodmin Moor. It was built as a coaching inn for tired travellers in 1750 but became known in times gone by for its association with smugglers. During our stay, we visited the inn's fantastic museum. It is full of tools and artefacts used by smugglers, including lanterns, hooks, barrels and even a 200-year-old mummified mouse! You will read about some of these items in this book. I was so inspired by the museum that when I tried to go to sleep, I had to keep turning on the light to write down my ideas for the story. After waking my mum up for the sixth time, she did start to lose patience with me!

I put together all the ideas and inspiration from my trip with a modern twist – weaving into the story how the characters in the book could use DNA to find out secrets about the past, to bring families together and to solve a modern-day crime. I hope you enjoy reading this book as much as I enjoyed researching and writing it. Every time I sat down to write it it was like jumping back into my childhood holidays and a big smile would spread across my face.

So, find yourself a comfortable spot and get ready for a fantastic, page-turning story with many unexpected twists and turns. I hope you enjoy finding out about DNA, get as excited as the characters in discovering secret tunnels, hidden treasure and finding out about stories from the past, and maybe you can work out how the characters in the story can use DNA to solve a crime. I hope it inspires you with a love of science just as I was inspired those many years ago when I was in the laboratory and saw DNA for the first time!

I have created a series of web links to accompany many of the chapters in this book. If you follow these links you will be able to find out more about DNA, cells, forensic scientists, ship wreckers and smugglers, and even print out the evidence used by the characters in the book to see if you can solve the case!

You can also try some fun activities such as extracting DNA from fruit, making a DNA helix out of sweets, becoming a forensic scientist and collecting clues to solve an online case, having a go at DNA fingerprinting or even extracting some DNA in your own virtual laboratory!

Go to **www.thelittlestorytellingcompany.co.uk/ the-dna-detectives-the-smugglers-daughter** to access the weblinks for this book.

Chapter 1

Holiday time!

"Mum, tell us again. What did you say?" asked Annabelle. She was sure that she hadn't heard her mum properly and that she must be mistaken. She looked across at Harry who seemed equally confused.

"Please let it be true!" they both thought, crossing their fingers and feeling the fizz of excitement building in their tummies.

"We're all going on the Wallace family holiday tomorrow to a little out of the way place in Cornwall called Tresorporth. It means 'Treasure Cove' – and they accept dogs, so yes, Milly's coming too!" she repeated.

"Treasure Cove!" echoed Annabelle and Harry in unison. They danced round the kitchen together with Milly singing, "We're going on holiday! We're going on holiday!" Then they both stopped, remembering the other bit she had said.

"Did you say something about a secret tunnel?" said Harry.

"Oh you don't want to know about that, do you?" said Mum laughing. Harry smiled his cheeky smile at her and his green eyes shone. "Please tell me," he pleaded tipping his head to one side as he hugged his Mum really hard. Annabelle knew this was his ploy to get what he wanted and annoyingly Mum always seemed to fall for it.

"Okay! Get off, Harry! I've been asked to help with a project with Exeter University to collect DNA samples from local people who live in Cornwall. We're going use their DNA to try and find out where the local people originally came from many years ago. We're going to try and find out if they were Celtic – Celts were the tribes that lived in Cornwall during the Iron Age and Roman periods – or if they were Anglo-Saxon – a group of people who arrived after the Romans and came from European countries like Germany, Denmark and the Netherlands. Or maybe they came from somewhere else? I also want to show you the laboratory I used to work in when I worked at the hospital in Exeter. My old colleagues really want to meet you!"

"That's really exciting, Mum," said Annabelle. She loved hearing all about the projects her mum was working on. Most of the work her mum did was carried out in the laboratory she had in the garden.

Annabelle and Harry were often allowed to help her, although Harry currently seemed more interested in football and whether his new football trainers and shin pads had arrived in the post.

Annabelle was fascinated that our DNA, the instructions needed to make a human being, could actually be used to find out where in the world you came from. She wondered what her DNA would say about her. She knew her dad's side of the family came from Ireland and America. She wondered if the scientists would be able to tell that if they looked at her DNA. Would it reveal another country that the family didn't know about? Was she descended from the Anglo-Saxons? She would quite like to be a Viking as they were learning about the Vikings at school. Her thoughts were interrupted by an impatient outburst from Harry:

"Mum, tell us about the tunnel!"

"Well, I don't know if it's true. But the area was a well-known haunt in the past for smugglers and ship wreckers. The wreckers, according to the stories, used to put lanterns or 'false lights' onto the rocks late at night. The ships would think they were coming into a harbour, but really, the lights would lead them into areas where the rocks would be incredibly treacherous. The ships would be shredded. The waiting men would plunder – that means steal – the goods from the ship. They didn't want to be seen by the coastguard as they would be arrested so they needed to get off the beach as quickly as possible. At Tresorporth there is said to be a smuggler's tunnel that leads from the beach to the church up on the cliffs. According to my friends who live there no one has ever found it, though. Although plenty of people have looked! Apparently there's also supposed to be treasure from one of the ships that was wrecked that has never been found either. That's why it's called Tresorporth – 'Treasure Cove'."

Harry and Annabelle listened to her intently and excitedly. Then Harry rushed out of the kitchen at breakneck speed. Annabelle and her Mum looked up at the ceiling as they heard his feet hammering up the stairs. He shouted, "I'm off to pack!" Annabelle heard the footsteps stomping into her room and ran upstairs after him to see what he was up to.

Harry was standing in her room and was a very comical sight. In the short space of time he had got a head torch, which was switched on, and he was wearing it on his head. Around his shoulder he had some binoculars and he had Annabelle's torches which he was about to steal, in both hands.

"Those are mine!" said Annabelle, snatching them off him.

"We need to be prepared, Annabelle. We're going to find the Smuggler's Tunnel *and* the treasure! Don't forget, we're the 'DNA Detectives'. No challenge is too great for us!"

Annabelle smiled at her younger brother. She looked across at her notice board. Proudly pinned up in the centre was the newspaper article from their last adventure, when she and Harry had become the "DNA Detectives". The two of them had used DNA and collected evidence, just like real detectives, to catch the local pet thief who had stolen their pet dog

Milly and their friend's dogs. She remembered the moment they had been reunited with Milly and a big smile filled her face. Surely, if they could solve that mystery, they could find a tunnel on a beach. How hard could it be?

"Shall I pack our 'DNA Detectives' kit, Harry?"

Harry smiled.

"Definitely! I think we're going to need it! I'm so excited. Mum said we're going to set off really early tomorrow. I can't wait for Dad to get home from work so I can tell him all about it!"

Just one more sleep, Annabelle thought as she patted Milly, and the adventure would begin.

Chapter 2

A discovery on the beach

I t had been a long journey down to Cornwall, but as the car turned the corner from up on the cliffs they were all rewarded with the most incredible view of Tresorporth down in the valley. Annabelle could see a collection of beautiful little white cottages surrounding the most gorgeous little cove and a small sandy beach. She could see fishing boats bobbing about in the turquoise water which sparkled in the sunlight. As she looked across from the cove she could see a church up on the cliffs, overlooking the beach.

"Mum, listen to the seagulls! They're so noisy!" said Annabelle as Dad opened the sun roof. Annabelle could see them flying overhead.

"I know," said Mum, "and the road is so narrow and twisty. Go slowly!" she urged Annabelle and Harry's Dad. Annabelle looked out of the car to be greeted with what seemed to be a meadow of flowers brushing past her window. She could see cow parsley, foxgloves and she was sure that was red campion. Milly climbed over Harry and sniffed at the window, waking him up. He rubbed his eyes and shouted, "I can see the sea! Did I beat Annabelle?" They always had a competition to see who could see the sea first. She always let Harry win.

Annabelle could see why this would be a great place for smugglers. It was in the middle of nowhere. The nearest village was over three miles away and the rocks around the little cove looked really rugged. She could imagine how easily a ship would get wrecked on those rocks if it got drawn off course.

"Mum, are we there yet? Can we go to the beach? Please!" shouted Harry, desperately. All he wanted to do was find the smuggler's tunnel. He wished Dad would just park so they could get out and explore.

"Come on!" he thought to himself.

"Please be patient, Harry. We need to get to the holiday cottage first!" said Mum. Annabelle thought Mum sounded weary. Harry had talked about smugglers and secret tunnels for the entire journey, apart from the final 20 minutes when he had fallen asleep and snored really loudly. Annabelle couldn't wait to go and explore the little cove either. But she kept quiet. She knew Mum and Dad were tired after the long journey.

"We're here at last!" said Dad. They pulled into a small car park and Harry jumped out immediately.

"It's beautiful," said Annabelle. She stared at the beautiful white-walled cottage in front of her. It had a thatched roof, a very old front door and stone windowsills. There looked like there had been a sign at one point over the door and the garden led down to a stone wall which overlooked the beach. Mum and Dad unlocked the door and disappeared inside the cottage.

"We're so lucky! A holiday cottage right by the beach," said Annabelle. She breathed in the smell of the sea air. Her heart fluttered with excitement.

Mum shouted from the house. "Come and look – there is a welcome letter addressed to the Wallace Family. You might want to have a look at the information book that goes with the cottage. It says there are surf lessons on the beach!" Annabelle ran inside to look.

"Mum! Quick! We need to go down to the beach now!" shouted Harry. He was hanging dangerously over the wall. On the other side was a long drop down to the beach below. "The tide's just going out. We'll be the first to fish the rock pools if we go now." The beach looked amazing and Harry could see lots of gaps in the rock that could be a hiding place for a smuggler's tunnel. Leaning out he had a great view of the cliffs.

"Harry, get away from that wall now!" shouted Mum anxiously as she came out of the cottage. But Harry had already disappeared somewhere else.

"Please, Mum. Can we go to the beach?" said Annabelle "I'll look after Harry, and Milly could do to stretch her paws!"

"Okay. We'll unpack the car and then come down to find you. Hold on – I will get the nets and crab lines."

"Already got it!" said Harry. They all looked round at him. He had his head torch on his head, a bucket, crab lines and a fishing net in one hand, and a torch in the other. He did look ready for action! They all laughed.

"Come on, Annabelle. I'll race you to the beach! Later, parents!" shouted Harry as he ran off. At last!

Annabelle ran after Harry, trying to keep up with him. His legs must have grown again. Luckily, with Milly pulling so hard on the lead, desperate to follow Harry, she managed to catch up.

"These rock pools are amazing, Harry. Look, the tide is just going out, so I bet there'll be even more soon."

"Are you mad? We're here to find the smuggler's tunnel," said Harry. "We need to check every bit of these cliffs. We'll find it. I know we will. It won't be obvious though. We need to check behind rocks and in these gullies."

He gave Annabelle the bucket, net and crab lines. She watched him leaping away from her at great speed over the rocks. She could also see that the seaweed on the rocks made them slippery and the barnacles made them sharp. He would definitely fall at some point.

"Look at Milly," said Annabelle, pointing at the little dog. Milly jumped confidently into a rock pool, expecting it to be shallow. The depth surprised her and her head suddenly disappeared under the water. She had to swim to the other side. The expression on her face was hilarious; one of utter shock. Both children collapsed laughing. Milly wagged her tail. Her black curly fur was soaking which made her look really skinny. She shook herself all over the children and that made them laugh even more!

Harry turned away to continue with his quest. This was the best! He found if he leapt from rock to rock he could get where he wanted even quicker.

"Harry, slow down! The rocks are slippery," warned Annabelle. She loved the dramatic shapes formed by the dark grey granite rocks. They seemed to slice through the ground and then poke up high into the sky around the little beach. As the tide went out further, more rocks were revealed. She could see why this cove must have been deceptive to a ship's crew. From above, it looked like the bottom of the sea was sandy, but actually the sand was hiding more deadly sharp rocks. It really was a ship wrecker's perfect spot, Annabelle decided. Remote and deadly!

"Aaaaagh!" a high-pitched cry filled the air.

"Harry, are you okay?" shouted Annabelle. She watched Milly run as fast as she could to where Harry had fallen. The little dog licked his face, which made him giggle.

"Get off Milly! I'm fine! I slipped and cut my knee. You have to come quickly though, I've just seen the *biggest* crab I have ever seen in my whole life. That's why I slipped – I was rushing to get it before it got away! I think it might be one of those edible crabs

Dad showed us at the market. Quick, come on, it's huge! Milly, get out of the pool, you'll scare him!"

Annabelle wasn't sure she wanted to see a huge crab. That meant it had huge claws, which might pinch you. As she got closer the sun came out from behind a cloud. She watched as the light hit the rock pool. She and Harry both saw something catch the light. It glimmered in the bottom of the rock pool.

"What's that?" exclaimed Harry. The rock pool was quite deep but, before Annabelle could warn Harry not to, he had leapt into the pool. His shorts were wet through but she knew he wouldn't care.

"What is it, Harry?"

Harry could feel his wet shorts, cold and damp against his skin but he ignored it. He picked up the object and brought it quickly to the surface. He held it up for them to see.

"It's a locket!" they both exclaimed.

"I wonder how it got here," said Annabelle.

"I think it must have been washed up from the shipwreck Mum told us about. Maybe there was a storm just before we got here... or *maybe* the smugglers dropped it, and it's been in this rock pool for all this time!"

Annabelle took the locket from Harry and held it in her hand. "It's so pretty. Look at the little bird on the front. Do you think it's made of gold?"

"I know it's made of gold, Annabelle!" said Harry, snatching it back. "Look at the little flower next to the bird. It must have taken ages to make all the details. I can even see the veins in the leaves. Look, there's a sparkling blue diamond in the centre. Get off Milly, you can't have it!" He pushed the curious little dog away.

"I think that's a sapphire!"

"It must be really valuable. I think the chain's made of gold too. Hold on, look, there's something written on the back."

"What does it say? Hurry up, Harry," said Annabelle. She could hardly contain her excitement.

"It says 'My darling little Elise – born 8th March 1871', that's, erm, hold on... 145 years ago! I *knew* it was old. Shall we open it?"

"Okay, Harry. But do it really carefully." They both gasped as the locket clicked open, revealing a black and white photo.

"It looks really old," whispered Annabelle. "It's faded but you can tell it's a girl. I think she's about the same age as me. Do you think that's Elise?"

"It could be. Look on the other side. It looks like a lock of blond hair. This is so exciting. I bet that's Elise's hair. Remember Mum kept our hair when we first had it cut? She said it was our first curl and then she got all mushy about when we were babies. Maybe this is Elise's first curl? Come on Annabelle, let's go and show Mum and Dad!"

"Harry, stop. I've found something else! Look at these funny marks in the sand? What're they from, I wonder?"

"They're not like footprints, they're a funny shape. Hold on... do you think they might be from flippers?"

"Yes I think they are. And they're too big to be from a child. There are more here. Come on Harry, let's follow them!"

This time Annabelle led the way. She was really proud that, for once, Harry was listening to her.

"The prints are going into this gully. That's so clever... from the beach you wouldn't know this is here, because these rocks hide the entrance."

Harry climbed over the rocks with Milly following at his heels. Every now and then she would turn back and make sure Annabelle was close behind. Harry followed the prints towards the end of the gully, where there was a huge rock. Milly sniffed the ground along the gully then barked furiously at the rock. Her tail frantically wagged from side to side.

"I think she can smell something!" shouted Harry. "Maybe there's something behind the rock. I think it could it be the tunnel. It's really well hidden. You can't see it from the beach or even if you walked past. Come here, Annabelle. Help me to move it!"

"You are mad, Harry. I am not Superman."

"You mean Superwoman!"

"Whatever! I cannot move that rock, it's huge!"

Harry tried heroically to move the rock himself but with no luck. Annabelle found it hilarious watching him try – he was so determined!

He eventually gave in trying to move the rock and decided to climb on top instead. Milly stood on her back legs, longing to follow him, but it was too high. He switched on his head torch and tried to peer into the small crack between the cliff and the rock. With great excitement, Harry watched as the light from the torch continued into the rock and lit up what looked like a passageway.

"Annabelle! You're not going to *believe* this!"

Annabelle saw Harry's eyes were wide as saucers and a huge grin filled his face.

"I can see a tunnel!" he said.

"You're kidding. Do you think it's the smuggler's tunnel?"

"I *know* it is. I told you I would find it! Let's stack up some stones so we can mark where it is. We'll come back and find a way in. I think we should show

Mum and Dad the locket. But don't tell them about the tunnel. They'll never let us go in it. Promise you won't!"

"Okay. I promise I won't. Come on, Harry – I can't wait to show Mum and Dad the locket. They just won't believe it – what a first day! I knew this was going to be the start of an amazing adventure!"

Annabelle clasped the locket tightly in her hand. Could it really be from the shipwreck...? Or even dropped by the smugglers like Harry had said? Had they really found the smuggler's tunnel? It really was too exciting for words! Annabelle ran off after Harry to find Mum and Dad.

Chapter 3

The Museum

"I want chocolate!" shouted Harry.

"Strawberry for me please," said Annabelle quietly. The lovely old lady in the beach cafe took their orders.

"Ooh!" she exclaimed. "What have you got there, my love?" She had spotted the locket which the children were showing to their parents. Mum and Dad had agreed to buy Annabelle and Harry an ice cream to celebrate their exciting find!

"We found it in a rock pool," said Harry proudly.

"I think that must've been left by the smugglers!" said the lady, winking at the children's parents. "You should take it to the museum in the village. I bet they could tell you more about it. It's next to the post office near the market." She shuffled off to get the ice creams.

"Can we go after this? Please!" pleaded Harry. "I will eat my ice cream really fast, I promise!" He sneaked some of the cone to Milly under the table

29

who was delighted to help him out. She had only just finished eating some of Annabelle's!

"We just need to go and take Milly back to the cottage, Harry, then we can go," said Mum.
Both children cheered.

✳ ✳ ✳

The museum was in a beautiful building which, according to the plaque, used to be where they had built and repaired fishing boats for the village. To enter the museum you had to go through a small wooden door. It formed a section of two huge doors which would have had to be opened to get the boats in and out. The doors had been painted bright blue which looked very impressive against the white stone walls. Harry rushed ahead as always. When they caught up with him he was busy chatting to a lady behind the counter in the entrance. Annabelle could see the lady was listening to Harry with great interest. In her hand was the locket. Annabelle felt disappointed. She had wanted to be the one to show the locket to the museum staff. Maybe she could be the one to find out its secrets and find out who the girl in the photo was – yes, that would make up for it!

"Well, well, well! What an exciting thing to find," said the lady, smiling as Annabelle approached. "Your brother has been telling me all about this beautiful locket you found. My name is Alice." The lady must have been about the same age as their aunt Sarah. She had black glasses and her blonde hair was pulled back into a neat bun. Annabelle thought she had a kind smile, and she seemed very interested in what they had found.

"Do you think the locket was left by smugglers?" said Annabelle. Alice laughed and Annabelle felt a little hurt. "That's what the lady in the beach cafe told us," she added defensively. Alice sensed she had upset her and was keen to make amends: "The smuggling and wrecking in this village went on over 100 years ago. That's a long time for the locket to have been in the rock pool. Especially with all the children that come down and fish in those rock pools every day! I think it would have been spotted before. There's a shipwreck in the cove that was rumoured to contain treasure. Maybe it's washed up from there? We haven't had any storms lately, though. Sometimes things get washed up following a storm."

"Do you know any more about the ship that was wrecked?" asked the children.

"Well, it's a really interesting story. The ship set

sail from Norway with the crew and a very rich family on board in 1881. The head of the family owned the ship and was on board to set up business deals in Cornwall. He had brought his wife and young daughter with him." Annabelle nudged Harry at the mention of the young girl. He smiled excitedly at her, obviously thinking the same thing. Could it be Elise – the girl from the locket?

Alice continued: "They also had a cargo of timber to be sold in Cornwall in trade for tin from the tin mines. They were destined to sail to Falmouth but four days into their journey from Norway, apparently there was a terrible storm one night. They were looking for a harbour where they could shelter. They thought they'd reached a safe harbour as they saw lights, but it was a trick to lure them onto the sharp rocks you've probably seen on the beach. The hull of the ship was torn to shreds. Wreckers seized the goods from the ship before it sank. It's rumoured there were gold coins and jewellery from the family on board. But they were never found. Sadly the crew and all the members of the family drowned, except the young girl. She was saved by the wreckers and taken in by a local family. I don't really know any more about that, apart from that the family owned the local Inn. I think it's now a holiday cottage. It's in the centre of the village overlooking the cove."

"I bet that's our holiday cottage!" said Harry
excitedly. Annabelle thought it could be too. Her heart
leapt with excitement. Alice smiled as she listened to
the children.

"There's something about the history of the holiday
cottage written in the information book that comes
with the cottage. I didn't read it, did you?" Annabelle
asked Harry.

Harry shook his head. "No! I just wanted to find out
what TV channels there were. I bet it'll tell us whether
our holiday cottage used to be the old Inn."

"We must check as soon as we get back. I'm *sure*
we're staying in the place where Elise lived!" replied
Annabelle, her voice full of excitement.

Alice went on: "I believe the girl lived to a good
age and is buried somewhere in the churchyard up
on the cliffs."

"Do you know what the girl was called?" asked
Annabelle.

"I can't remember. I'm really sorry. It would be
worth you going to the library, though. They have
some books about local smugglers and ship wreckers.
They may also have details of the girl in the local
records. If you have a look there's a photo of the
shipwreck in the museum. You'll also find some

of the equipment used by the smugglers that was found locally."

Annabelle and Harry couldn't contain their disappointment that Alice couldn't remember the girl's name. That would have solved the mystery.

"I tell you what," said Alice, feeling sorry for the two children. "As long as it is okay with your parents why don't I take the locket and show it to our history experts. They might know how old it is and where it comes from. It's very unusual. Oh and hold on... there is something else..."

She rushed off into a back room. The children could hear lots of banging and crashing and things being moved. Seconds later she was back, clutching an old battered leather book in her hand.

"I just remembered. Some builders who were renovating the holiday cottage found this and some other items used by smugglers. We displayed the smuggler's tools in the museum but we weren't sure what to do with this. It's someone's diary. It is *very* old. Apparently the builders found it behind the fireplace in one of the rooms when they were taking the fireplace out. It had been hidden behind some of the bricks. The owners weren't interested in any of the bits and told the builders to get rid of it. So they brought it here. I haven't had chance to look at it but if your holiday cottage was the Old Inn you might find something useful in there. You must promise to bring it back and tell me if you find anything."

Annabelle and Harry nodded their heads furiously in response. Alice passed the old battered book to Annabelle.

"Thank you," Annabelle said, carefully accepting the book, and wondering if its contents might hold the clues to the little girl in the locket. All she wanted to do was read it, but she could see Harry had itchy feet. She tucked the diary into her pocket.

"I'll make sure they bring the book back. That's really kind of you. Thank you so much," said Mum. "Children, why don't you go and see if you can find the photo of the shipwreck."

Harry didn't need any encouragement. "Quick, come on!" he said, dragging Annabelle after him.

Annabelle was marvelling at all the interesting items in the museum. They were displayed in big old glass cases. Suddenly she spotted something disgusting. "Urghhh!" she screamed. "What is that?"

Harry read the sign. "It's a mummified mouse they found in the Old Inn – it's 150 years old!"

"That's disgusting. I hope our holiday cottage isn't the Old Inn if there are mice there!" said Annabelle, screwing up her face.

"Look at this!" said Harry, racing ahead.

Annabelle read the label: "A smuggler's bible. Wow! How cool is this.

'The smugglers made a block of wood into the shape of a bible. They hollowed out the back and put in a tin container which could be filled with brandy. Then the smuggler's wives could distribute the stolen brandy without being caught! They referred to stolen brandy using the code "Cousin Jack" so people wouldn't know what they were talking about.'"

She was amazed at how much the block of wood looked like a book. The smugglers were really clever!

"I like this," said Harry. "Apparently they would use a sack of potatoes to hide stolen goods. They would hollow out some of the potatoes, place the stolen goods inside. Then replace the skin with wire to hold it in place, wipe the surface over with soil to conceal the cut and put it in the sack with the other potatoes."

"Goodness, it must've taken ages to find the goods!" laughed Annabelle.

Harry was already off to the next exhibit, though.

"Look Annabelle, it's the ship!"

The children stared at a very old black and white photograph which showed the very ends of the masts of a ship sticking out of the water. They recognised the beach as Tresorporth. The shape of the rocks hadn't changed much. They hadn't seen any masts sticking out of the water. They must have rotted away or been broken in the storms and sunk to the bottom of the sea.

"It says 'Norwegian Ship *The Helena* wrecked during a storm at Tresorporth, March 1881,' said Annabelle. "If the ship was wrecked in 1881 and Elise was born in 1871 – like it says on the locket – that would make her 10 years old when the ship sank. We thought the girl in the photo was about the same age as me. That makes sense. I'm sure the locket is from the family that were on *The Helena*." She was thrilled they had managed to work it out.

"Let's see if there are any more clues," said Harry, running ahead again. "Annabelle, quick. Come and see what I've found!"

Annabelle ran as fast as she could to the next display case. It was full of old lanterns.

"These could be the lanterns they used to lure the ship onto the rocks," said Harry. "The lady said they were all found locally."

"Look – they could make this one flicker so they

could send messages to each other along the cliffs," said Annabelle.

"This one was called a 'Spout Lantern'," said Harry. "The spout was used so the light was only visible out to sea. You couldn't see it if you were on land which would have definitely given the game away! I love all this!"

There was a huge grin on his face. Annabelle thought he would have made a great smuggler. He was always sneaking sweets and food and hiding them in his room. Maybe this was not such a great thing – it could give him even more ideas!

"This is even more exciting, Annabelle," he said, ushering her to come quickly. "The smugglers used to hide their stolen goods down wells. This thing is an 'Old Spring Well Hook'. Apparently the smugglers would tie the goods on ropes and this thing here…" He pointed to a long black metal object with a rounded end. "The spring well hook would stop the rope slipping into the well."

Annabelle was relieved they didn't have a well at home as she was sure Harry would have tried that!

"I don't think there are any more clues here, Harry," she said, "and I really want to find out whether our holiday cottage is the Old Inn. We could be staying in the house where Elise lived when she was taken in by the local family. Let's go home now!"

"Me neither," said Harry jumping up and down with excitement. He ran over to their parents, who were enjoying looking around the museum. He pulled Mum and Dad towards the exit.

"What are you like, Harry?" said Dad. "First of all you're at us because you want to go to the museum and now you want to go home. Will you ever be happy?"

"No!" whispered Harry to Annabelle. "Not till we've found out where Elise lived! Let's go, Annabelle."

In all the excitement Annabelle had almost forgotten the diary. She felt in her pocket and touched the surface of the leather with her fingers. A sense of relief passed through her that it was still there. Bedtime reading was going to be very interesting tonight. She was sure the diary would hold the key to the mysterious locket and Elise.

Chapter 4

Who is the smuggler's daughter?

Annabelle and Harry wrestled over the information book, each wanting to read the section about the history first. The racket was deafening as they shouted and pulled and pushed one another, and it grew louder still when Milly started barking and jumping up at them both, not wanting to be left out.

"Enough!" shouted Mum, as she flung open the door and burst into the lounge. The sound of the door banging made the children and Milly stop what they were doing immediately. Annabelle and Harry watched in dismay as Mum took the book from them.

"*I* will read about the history of the cottage to you both, if it will stop you squabbling. Sit down!"

Milly was tucked in between the children, her head on Annabelle's lap. Annabelle could see she had what she called "Trouble eyes". This is when they looked really sad and the whites showed. Just like Annabelle, Milly hated getting told off. Harry, on the other hand, didn't look bothered at all!

"The book says this cottage used to be the village Inn for many years," said Mum, "and was called The Tresor Pot. That's interesting. We know 'Tresor' is Cornish for treasure. So this house was the treasure pot! I wonder if it was used to store treasure!" she laughed. "Oh wow. The landlord of the pub was called Henry Nance. He lived here with his family. It says it was rumoured that Henry Nance was the ringleader of a group of men who were involved in ship wrecking and smuggling."

Mum looked round at the children. You could have heard a pin drop. They were gazing wide eyed at her, hanging off her every word.

"Alice, the lady at the museum," said Annabelle, "told us a little girl was the only survivor from *The Helena*, the Norwegian ship that was wrecked at Tresorporth, and she was taken in by the family that lived in the local Inn. She came to live *here*! In our holiday cottage! I wonder if we're sleeping in her bedroom!"

"I don't want to sleep in a *girl's* bedroom," said Harry.

"Don't be silly, Harry!" said Mum, crossly.

"Can we go to the library, please, Mum?" said Annabelle. "The lady at the museum said we could find out more about the shipwreck there. We're sure the

42

little girl is the girl from the locket we found but we need proof! Please can we?"

"How can I resist those pleading faces," laughed Mum. "But please Annabelle, would you put that book the lady gave you somewhere safe first?"

Annabelle ran as fast as she could up the wooden stairs to their bedroom. She placed the diary carefully under her pillow and grabbed her notebook so she could record any useful information they found at the library. Bedtime reading would have to wait. They had to get to the library immediately!

✳ ✳ ✳

The library was a modern-looking building near to the small village primary school. The electric doors of the library flew open automatically as the children approached. They jumped back just as a man dressed like a vicar came out through the doors, in a hurry. He pushed his way past the children, scowling at them as he did. Then he hurried off around the corner and into the village.

"Hey! Watch out!" exclaimed Harry.

"I wonder why he was so grumpy?" said Annabelle.

"Maybe he's late for church?" Mum reassured them.

"Why don't you go and ask that man over there if there are any books on local ship wreckers or smugglers?"

The man looked up and came rushing over. He was young, with dark brown hair, glasses and lots of freckles on his nose. He looked really excited.

"Aren't you the children who found the locket on the beach?" he said.

"That's us!" said Harry, proudly. "We think it was left by the smugglers! The lady in the museum thinks it's very old!"

"How exciting! In that case, I know exactly the book you would like to see. Luckily it's just been returned this morning. There was an old lady looking for it yesterday too. She just moved back to the area and is researching her family tree. Yes, a very popular book! Follow me."

Annabelle and Harry followed the man to a shelf near the machines where you scan your books to bring them back or take them home. He was tall with long legs and the children had to walk really fast to keep up with him.

"*Smuggling and Ship Wrecking in Tresorporth* – here it is. It will tell you all about what went on in the Cove in the past." The man handed the book to the children.

"Thank you," said Annabelle. Harry snatched the book from her and ran to the nearest table. The book fell open.

"The pages are covered in grubby fingerprints," said Annabelle, pointing at them. "Why don't people wash their hands when they read a book? And look, the corners of the page have been *folded*. I think someone was interested in whatever is on that page..."

"Annabelle, look! Look at the photo!" shouted Harry, urgently.

"It's a ship!"

"Yes. I know it's a ship! It's *The Helena*. But look at the lady on board."

Annabelle looked at Harry who had gone unusually quiet. She looked closely at the photo.

"Oh my goodness. It's the locket. She's wearing the locket. You can see the bird and the flower really clearly. Look, she has her arms around a little girl – she looks identical to the girl in the photo! It *must* be Elise!"

Annabelle threw her arms around Harry in delight. She couldn't believe it was the same locket. But it really was. She could see with her own eyes.

"The book says this photo was taken before *The Helena* set sail from Norway heading for Falmouth," Annabelle read aloud to Harry, whose eyes were sparkling with excitement. "It's just like the lady in the museum told us the family were very rich and the father owned the boat. My goodness, look – there's a list of all the jewels that were on board that belonged to the mother, and apparently the cargo contained gold coins and timber..."

Annabelle ran her finger down the list of jewellery.

"Harry, this must be it – a locket, with the picture of a bird and a flower on the front, made of gold and sapphires. The locket was *definitely* on board *The Helena* when it sank. But how did it end up in the rock pool?"

She wrote "locket listed in cargo on board *The Helena*" in her notepad.

"Look, Annabelle," said Harry. "It says here:

'It was rumoured that the ship was drawn onto the rocks by the landlord of the local inn, The Tresor Pot, and his gang of men on a dark, stormy night in March 1881.'

"We know the landlord was called Henry Nance from the information book.

'Old stories that have been passed down by local families say the sea that night had been perilous. The men in the gang had put lanterns onto the rocks to make passing ships think they had found a safe harbour. As The Helena steered towards

the lights her hull was torn to shreds on the sharp rocks that line Tresor Cove. The men waiting on the shore sailed out to the stricken ship in small boats and stole much of the cargo before the ship sank. Many say the vicar at the time was involved with the gang and helped them to hide the goods from the coastguard. Timbers from The Helena can be found in the Old Inn in Tresorporth. The whereabouts of the tunnel, jewellery and gold coins has never been discovered. Locals believe the jewels and coins may still be on the wreck or hidden somewhere in the village. All onboard drowned, apart from a young girl who was taken in by the landlord Henry Nance and his family.'"

"Oh wow, Harry! What an incredible story. Amazing to think how the story has been passed down over generations. I wonder where the jewels are now and how we can find out more about the landlord of The Tresor Pot and his family. I've written it all down in my notepad."

"Sssh! Be quiet, Annabelle. Don't look up now but we are being watched. I think the man from the library who helped us earlier and his friend are listening to us. I've been watching them. They keep chatting and then pointing at us."

Annabelle looked up. The two men waved at her and came over.

"Found anything interesting?" said the tall man who had helped them when they arrived.

"Not really," said Harry, doing his best to look bored.

Annabelle turned over her notepad, and asked the men, "How can we find out more about people who lived in the village a long time ago?"

"You'll need to look at the census," said the second man. He had ginger hair and stared at the two children. They could see he was trying to read what was in the book over their shoulder. Annabelle snapped the book closed. The man seemed to jump.

"What's a census?" asked Harry.

"Well, every ten years since 1801, and even today, a record has been made of all the households and people living in the country. Records were made of someone's address, name, whether they were married or single, age at last birthday, male or female, job, and place of birth. Follow me and I'll show you where they are kept."

The children followed excitedly. They couldn't wait to look through the records and find out more about Henry Nance and his family.

The man took the children to another part of the library. The light flickered on.

"Our records go back to 1801," said the man

proudly. "I'll have to supervise you if you want to look at the records. What's it you are looking for?"

He seemed to nod to the other man.

"I wonder why they're so interested in what we're doing," whispered Harry.

Annabelle shrugged. "We wanted to find out about the family who lived in the holiday cottage we're staying in, when it was the local pub. We need the records for 1871, please," she asked.

The man pulled out a huge old black book labelled "1871 Census" in gold letters.

"Why 1871?" said Harry

"1871 was the time before the landlord took in the girl. She shouldn't be on the records then. The next census was in 1881, ten years later. According to these records the census was taken in April. We know *The Helena* sank in March so Elise, if she is the girl who was taken in by the landlord, should be listed in that census."

"This is so exciting! Quick, Annabelle, let's find the right page," said Harry.

The children scanned the list of names from 1871.

"Look for 'Henry Nance'," said Annabelle, "that was the name of the landlord." She was desperate to find it before Harry.

"Got it!" announced Harry. Annabelle looked

where his finger was pointing. She could see the details written in curly handwriting and black ink. The paper it was written on was so old it had become discoloured.

"Look!" said Annabelle. "'Henry Nance' – the address is listed as The Tresor Pot Inn. He's listed as married to Jenny Nance. 33 years old. His job is listed as 'landlord' and he was born in Tresorporth. He's got two children: Gwen, a baby girl aged six months and Jago, a boy aged two years. No mention of an Elise... as we thought!"

Annabelle turned to the man, who seemed fascinated with what she and her brother were doing, and asked, "Can we look at the 1881 census records please?" The children watched as the man returned the book for 1871 and found the record for 1881.

"Same again, Harry! Look for Henry Nance," said Annabelle. This time she was determined to find his information before Harry did. Her eyes scanned the page quickly looking for "Henry". There he was. "Got it!" she announced, pointing her finger to the name. Although she hardly dared look to see if Elise's name was there.

"Look – Henry is listed as 43 years old. He's still the landlord and listed as living in The Tresor Pot Inn. He's married, but hold on... he's listed as having three children! Jago is 12 years old, Gwen is 10 years old and now there is an Elise... who is also 10 years old! It must be our Elise!" shouted Annabelle.

"It can't be Henry's child or she would be listed in the 1871 census. It must be Elise, the only survivor from *The Helena* and the girl from the locket!" said Harry.

Annabelle wrote in her notepad: "proof, Elise is the girl from the locket, taken in by Henry Nance and his family from local Inn." She was just underlining the name Elise when the man peered at the children over his glasses.

"I couldn't help overhearing you talk about Henry Nance. I've got an article to show you which I think you'll find interesting. I was just making a copy for Alice at the museum. She asked me to research interesting articles about smugglers in the area."

"Maybe he's trying to help us after all," whispered Annabelle.

"I don't trust him," said Harry. "There's something odd about the way him and his friend keep looking at us."

Sensing the children's unease the man signalled the children to follow him to the photocopier. "Have a read of this," he said, and left them to it.

"It's a newspaper clipping from *The Cornish*

Times. The date is 1st April 1881, a month after *The Helena* sank," said Annabelle. "It says Henry Nance has been arrested by Customs Officers and was tried for smuggling and for putting out false lights to deliberately wreck *The Helena*. The court, however, was forced to dismiss the case due to lack of witnesses and the heroic act whereby Henry saved the life of Elise Andersdatter, the only survivor from the stricken ship. The court understands that Elise has been adopted into the family of Henry Nance and is currently residing in Tresorporth. The court made it clear to all present that anyone caught smuggling or setting out false lights to deliberately wreck ships risked prison, being sent to the colonies in Australia or death as punishment."

"Wow... he was lucky to escape from that one," said Harry. "It sounds like they were giving him a stern warning. Do it again and your time will be up! I wonder if he did carry on smuggling. His wife must've been cross with him for nearly getting caught. I would *never* get caught if I was a smuggler. Mum never catches me!"

Annabelle laughed.

"It depends if you leave evidence like the sweet wrappers under your duvet and the mouldy apple cores Mum found behind the TV! Come on, we can use our library cards in this library, let's take the book out so we can read it again when we get home."

"There you are!" said Mum. "I've been looking for you everywhere. I just bumped into two men who run the surf club. They said if you come down to the beach tomorrow you can have a lesson. They're really nice. I might ring my friend Paula who lives here and see if her children want to come too."

Annabelle and Harry high fived each other. This really was the best holiday ever. They had just proved that the girl from the locket was Elise and she had lived in their holiday cottage when it was the local pub. The landlord Henry Nance, it seemed, could very well have been involved in ship wrecking and sinking the ship Elise was on. Maybe the diary might be able to tell them more... But who did it belong to? Annabelle couldn't wait to get home. This time she dragged Harry out of the library and they ran as fast as they could to get back to the holiday cottage.

It was time to get some answers!

Chapter 5
A diary of secrets

(A)nnabelle worried that Mum and Dad might be suspicious of how willingly she and Harry had gone to bed that night. It was the first night of the holiday and usually, with their levels of excitement at fever pitch, Harry would try any excuse he could to stay up – he needed a drink, he needed the bed sheets to be tucked in, he had lost a toy, it was too light or too dark, he needed the toilet or he just needed to tell Mum and Dad something *really important*! It was unheard of for both children to voluntarily put on their pyjamas, clean their teeth and to want to read quietly to themselves.

Harry hadn't made a fuss about sleeping in a "girls'" room either, despite whinging earlier when he thought they might be staying in Elise's old bedroom. Annabelle hadn't moaned about sharing the room with Harry and how awful it would be because he snored like a warthog.

"I think if Mum and Dad hadn't been so tired we wouldn't have got away with this, Harry," she said, smiling. They chuckled as they heard Dad's snores. He had already fallen asleep on the sofa, tired after the long drive down to Tresorporth.

"Quick, Annabelle, get the diary. I can't wait to read it," said Harry, shutting the door so they wouldn't be overheard. Annabelle carefully retrieved the book from under her pillow.

"Let's get into my bed and read it," Annabelle suggested. She preferred that; she didn't really want to get into Harry's bed. He was always covered in dirt from whatever he had been up to in the day. She saw how much sand had been on his feet from the beach and he seemed to be constantly doing what he called "trouser explosions" under the duvet. Yes. It was much better this way!

Harry watched excitedly as Annabelle opened the first page of the battered old book. The handwriting was beautiful and written in black ink.

Annabelle started reading:

"This is the diary of... Elise Andersdatter! I have been given this book so I can write down my thoughts and try to make sense of the terrible fate that has been dealt to me. I don't know where to

start with the events of yesterday or whether, if I do,
they will ever make sense."

Harry grabbed hold of Annabelle and shook her.
"It's Elise's diary! Oh my goodness, Annabelle – it's her
diary! Quick, read on! I want to know what happened."
Annabelle smiled at Harry and then continued
to read:

"Tuesday, March 15th, 1881.
This day started out as the best day I think I ever
had. A few days earlier my mother and father and
I had set out from our home city of Bergen on the
west coast of Norway. My mother is English and
my father is Norwegian. I'm lucky I can speak and
write two languages! My father was taking us upon
his new ship The Helena which he named after my
mother. We're off to Cornwall in England to see if
my father can make new business contacts to sell
timber. My mother just wants to return to her home
in Falmouth to visit her friends and family. It's so
long since we have seen them.
    To celebrate our journey and bring us luck my
father has given my mother the most beautiful
locket and me a lucky penny which I wear in a purse
around my neck. The locket has a photo of me in it

taken on my 10th birthday just a few days ago and a lock of my hair which mother has kept since I was born! What a funny thing to keep! There's a lovely bird on the front and a flower with a sapphire of the deepest blue – the colour of the ocean – set into it.

As we sailed nearer to the Cornish coast a terrible storm blew up around us. I felt the ship start to rock increasingly violently as the waves got bigger and bigger. I've never seen such large waves which to me felt like mountains. As we rose steeply to the top of one wave the ship was thrown backwards then violently forwards down the next wave. It made me feel sick. The ride was never-ending. Each time the wave hit a shower of water broke over the bow, drenching the deck.

As night came and the darkness appeared there was no sign of the storm easing. The rain drove down in torrents lashing the ship. I heard the captain shout to my father that we needed to seek shelter. It was then we saw the lights on the shore. I thought with relief we had found safety. I felt the ship turn and head for the light. Just before we reached what we thought was safety, there was the most horrific grinding noise and juddering below us. I know now that was the sound of *The Helena* getting caught upon the sharp rocks at Tresorporth.

The rocks ripped into the hull and split the wood apart as if it was made of butter.

The ship creaked and groaned as water filled the lower decks. The Helena tipped slowly over onto her side. I ran up onto the deck and saw to my surprise that six, maybe seven small boats were rowing out to us filled with men. Their faces seemed to be blacked out and I couldn't see what they looked like even as they got closer. I know now that these men were ship wreckers and they blacked out their faces to avoid being seen. Innocently, however, as the rain lashed my face, and the wind howled around the sinking ship I thought, "Thank goodness these men are coming to save us!"

I saw some of the ship's crew had fallen into the cruel ocean but the men in the boats ignored their pleas for help. They rowed straight past them towards the ship wanting to get to the cargo before the ship sank. My mother and father were now up on deck. I waved at them and my mother waved back. She blew me a kiss. I watched as a wave crashed into the ship and swept them both overboard. It was the last time I saw them.

The men in the boats boarded the ship and swiftly unloaded the cargo of timber and brandy into their boats. They struggled with the barrels which, now waterlogged, were bulky and cumbersome. Their hands were wet and slippery. Other men picked up debris from The Helena floating in the water. Anything of value was hauled up into the boats. I was so cold and frightened, my clothes were drenched. By now I could feel the ship was sinking. I felt myself falling and someone grabbed me but I think I must have passed out. When I came round I was in one of the boats and had no recollection of how I got there. I watched with horror as The Helena sank, the masts sticking eerily out of the water. There were six men in my boat. They looked terrifying with their faces covered in black and their heavy boots. The gale howled about us, drowning out the noise of the remaining crew pleading to be saved. There was a man in my boat who seemed to be the ringleader. I know now this was Henry Nance. He barked orders at the men, shouting to be heard above the wind. The waves crashed about us with water spilling into the boat at frequent intervals. I was thrown a blanket by the ringleader. Although terrified, I was grateful for some warmth – I was shivering uncontrollably as we got nearer to the shore.

The boats were pulled up onto the beach crunching in the sand as they were drawn up away

from the clasps of the dark ocean. We were met
by black horses which were loaded up to carry the
goods to the cliffs. The horses' hooves made no
sound as they trotted through the sand; there was
just the sound of their breath and the clank
of the bridles as they were led away with their
cargo. I could make out the shapes of the men in
the darkness carrying goods towards the cliffs.
I watched the men fixing two poles through a loop in
a chain. They placed the heavy brandy barrels onto
the chains and then, balancing the poles on their
shoulders, carried the barrels up the beach. The men
groaned as the heavy weight was lifted onto their
shoulders. I was picked up and taken off the boat by
one of the men. He pushed me to join the line of men
travelling up the beach.

The speed at which the men worked and cleared
the goods off the beach was astonishing. I noticed a
man with a branch attached to a pole. He followed
behind the last horse, wiping away the prints from
the sand. Another walked by his side, making false
hoof prints with a metal branding iron in the sand.
I could see the false hoof prints were pointing in the
opposite direction of the real prints. If the customs
officers were to come now they would think the
horses had headed towards the sea and not in the

opposite direction! Instructions between the men were kept to a minimum. Each man seemed to know his role and all I could hear was the sound of the wind and the waves breaking onto the beach.

I looked at the sky. It had lightened and I sensed that dawn was just around the corner. The light, I suspected, would not be good for this group of men and there was an urgency about their business. Soon word would pass that a ship had been wrecked in the cove and this beach, despite its isolated position, would be swarming with customs officers who would arrest anyone they caught taking goods from the ship. My father had often told me about the harsh penalties for anyone stealing from a shipwreck and for putting out false lights to deliberately wreck a ship.

We climbed down into a gully. My wet hands were slippy against the rocks, making it hard to climb. Ahead of me I could see the men and the horses were going into a tunnel cut into the cliff. It hadn't been possible to see the tunnel from the beach. It was hidden away in the gully. As I entered the tunnel I saw a huge boulder had been moved aside to allow us to pass."

"It's the tunnel we found, Annabelle!" cried Harry, bouncing up and down with excitement. "I knew there would be a way in. She mentioned a gully just like the one we found and that huge boulder. That's *definitely* the one we found. We've found the secret smuggler's tunnel – I knew it!" "Sssh! Harry – Mum will hear you. I want to find out what happens next!"

Annabelle turned the page; she was desperate to find out what happened to Elise next. The poor girl. What a frightening ordeal. She continued to read:

"After what seemed a relatively short time we climbed through a wooden door and found ourselves in a stone-walled building with a high ceiling. I could see bells in the roof at the very top. The door was open and when I went through it I could see we were in a church. I was pushed towards the door, but not before I had seen the men had lifted the floorboards in the aisle leading to the altar and were hiding the goods underneath them. All under the guidance of the vicar!

I was pushed outside and saw more men in the graveyard. In the dawn's early light I could see they'd pushed open the lid of what I assume was a well. It was near to a statue of an angel and was flat on the ground. Not sticking out of it like some wells are. The men had a long black tool which they'd attached the stolen goods to and were lowering it down the well. The man I'd seen in the boat came storming over and got up close to my face. He whispered angrily, "You ain't seen nothin', right, young lady? If you want a home and to stay with me, you say nothin' if you know what is good for you." He dragged me away by the arm and back to my new home, The Tresor Pot Inn.

Henry Nance terrifies me. But I don't have much to do with him. Jenny his wife is really kind to me. I think she feels sorry for me and I get on really well with Gwen and Jago the two children. Maybe because we are so close in age. My bedroom had quite a few rotten floorboards. Henry has used the timber from The Helena to patch them up. I suppose most people wouldn't like that. But it makes me feel closer to mother and father. A little something to remember them by. Of course I still have my lucky penny. It was the only thing I had left from that awful night. It was kept safe in the purse around my neck. Maybe it's lucky and that's why I survived and was rescued. My bedroom is in the front of the inn and from the window I can see out to sea. As I look around my room it reminds me of home in Norway. The wallpaper is full of yellow flowers like the countryside where I come from. At this time of year the forests are full of these beautiful pale yellow flowers that

Norwegians call 'Kusymre'. They are my favourite flower. My mother calls them primroses. It was her favourite flower when she lived in Cornwall."

"Wow, Harry, what a story!" said Annabelle, closing the book. "She must have been terrified. I think that could be our bedroom. We're at the front of the cottage and we can see the sea from our window."

"I'm going to pull off some of this wallpaper to see," said Harry. He jumped off the bed with a big thud and was just about to rip away some of the wallpaper below the window when he heard Mum shouting up the stairs, "Go to bed now or no surf lesson in the morning. Now, Harry!"

"How did she know it was me?" he said. "I really want to see if there are yellow flowers."

"Don't, Harry, or Mum will stop us going surfing tomorrow. You know she will. Let's do it as soon as we wake up. Why don't we see if there's any wallpaper we can tear off under the bed so no one will see?"

"Good thinking, Annabelle. You know everything. Quick – the sooner we go to sleep the sooner it will be morning and we can find out if this was Elise's bedroom."

It was so hard to sleep knowing the answer to their burning question was just a fingertip away. But they would have to wait!

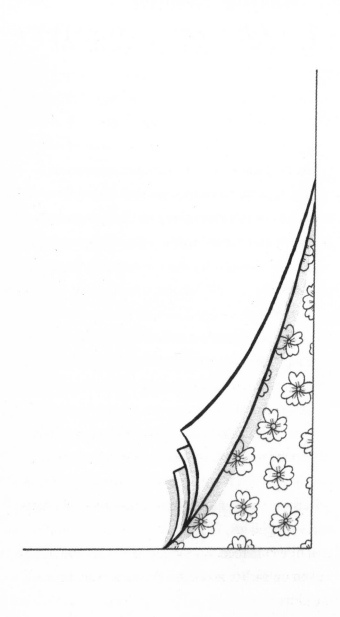

Chapter 6
Layers of wallpaper

Annabelle awoke to a scratching noise followed by someone ripping paper. A glance across at Harry's empty bed revealed the source of the noise and immediately she realised what he was up to. She quickly put her head over the side of the bed.

"Well?"

"There are three layers of wallpaper under this one. But the very last layer is..."

She watched Harry do a fake drum roll.

"Tell me! Is it or not?"

"It is! Yellow flowers just like Elise described. We're sleeping in Elise's bedroom and these very floorboards I'm lying on must be from *The Helena*!

Harry proudly shuffled out from under the bed and switched off his head torch. A huge satisfied grin filled his face. Annabelle felt cross she hadn't woken up earlier and then she could have got the glory.

Angrily she said, "Well, that means you're sleeping in a girl's bedroom!" As soon as she said it she felt really bad. He could just be so annoying sometimes.

"I don't care. I want to be in the same room as the timbers from a shipwreck. It's exciting," said Harry, peering down to look at them. "They do look really old. I can't believe they came all the way from Norway. Look at the wall here. The bricks are a different colour. That must have been where the old fireplace was. So the builders must have found Elise's diary there."

"Sorry Harry. I didn't mean to say that."

"That's okay. I think we should get dressed. Look out of the window – there are loads of surfers in the cove. It looks brilliant fun. I can't wait for our surf lesson! Mum's friend's children are having a lesson too. I hope they're cool. I was thinking we could go to the beach before the lesson and see if we could get into the tunnel. I'm going to put the detective kit in my bag in case we find something."

"Great idea, Harry! Come on, I'll race you to get dressed first!"

Annabelle felt relieved her horrible comment was all forgotten. That was the brilliant thing with Harry – he got over being wronged very quickly and was then onto the next thing!

*** *** ***

As they were walking to the beach Harry spotted a bakery. The smells coming from there were incredible and Annabelle realised, despite having breakfast, how hungry she was.

Annabelle watched as Harry dragged Mum into the shop. As she followed them inside, the vicar they had previously seen at the library was coming out. He looked angrily at Annabelle and pushed past her, before walking briskly away towards the church.

"Don't worry about him, my love!" said the man behind the counter "He's having a bad day."

"He's always having a bad day," laughed the other man. They were very friendly young men with strong Cornish accents. Annabelle liked the way they pronounced the words and always finished their sentences with "My love" which made you feel very welcome. She looked outside where Dad was waiting with Milly. The little dog had her nose in the air, sniffing the amazing smells coming from the shop.

"Now, what would you all like my lovelies? The doughnuts are just fresh out of the oven in the back or we have some amazing homemade pasties."

"My mum is obsessed with doughnuts!" said Harry,

laughing. Mum looked embarrassed. She did love
a doughnut!

"Would you all like one? I'll get one for Dad too,"
said Mum. Annabelle and Harry nodded their heads.
Annabelle thought they must have inherited their
love of doughnuts from Mum. They'd heard the story
so many times of when Mum had a doughnut and had
expected that gorgeous taste of the jam as she ate it
but it never came. Someone had forgotten to put the
jam in and Mum, it seemed, was outraged and had
never got over it.

"They do have jam in, don't they?" asked Annabelle
smiling. Mum gave her hand a squeeze
of appreciation.

"Of course, my love. Homemade jam too! Hold
on – I'll just get them from out the back. Aren't you
the children who found the locket on the beach?
Someone said it had a sapphire in it. Is that right?"

"Yes, and we think it was made of gold," said Harry,
proudly.

"Imagine that. Finding treasure like real pirates.
What did you do with it?" enquired the smaller of the
men as he put the doughnuts into a bag and handed
over the change.

"We gave it to the lady in the museum," said
Annabelle wondering how they had heard about it

and why they were asking so many questions.

"Will they give it back to you when they've finished with it?"

"I don't know. Mum I think we need to go or we'll miss our surf lesson," said Annabelle, grabbing Harry and making a hasty exit from the shop. The men looked shocked they had left so quickly. But as Annabelle walked away she could see they had their heads together and they were deep in conversation with each other. Was it about them? Why were they so interested in the locket? Harry didn't seem to care – he was running full pelt down the hill to the beach. Dad was being pulled by Milly after him. It was a very comical sight!

As they got nearer the beach, Annabelle could see Harry chatting to two lifeguards.

"Annabelle, this is Billy and Adam,' said Harry. "They're the lifeguards. Apparently the currents are really strong today, so we've got to be careful."

"We haven't seen you before. Are you on holiday here?" asked Adam, the taller of the two men.

"We're staying at the old Inn," said Mum.

"Oh. Are you the children that found the locket?" asked Billy, who had blond hair.

"That's us," said Harry. He really was so proud that everyone was asking them about it. But Annabelle wondered how word had got around so quickly.

"So where is it now?" asked Adam. He pushed his sunglasses over his head so he could look at them. Both men were wearing wetsuits. There were rescue aids and binoculars on the table in front of them.

"We gave it to the lady at the museum." Before Harry could say anything more Annabelle pulled him away.

Billy shouted after them, "Have you found the smuggler's tunnel yet?" Both men laughed as the children headed off in the direction of the rock pools.

"Annabelle, make sure you and Harry are back here for 10 o'clock for your surf lesson," shouted Mum. "Don't be late and watch Harry doesn't run over the rocks. We'll meet you here!"

"Do you think they know we've found the tunnel?" said Harry, looking worried.

"I don't know. But I think it's strange that so many people know about the locket and want to know where it is. So far, that is the men from the library, the boys in the bakery and now the lifeguards."

"Hold on, where's Milly off to? Milly, come here! Quick, Harry, run after her. See where she's going!"

Annabelle watched the little black dog running across the rocks. Milly was definitely on the scent of something and seemed to be heading for the smuggler's tunnel. When Annabelle caught up Harry seemed very excited. He was sitting where they had stacked up the stones near the gully and Milly was sitting cuddled up next to him.

"You're not going to believe it!" said Harry, his eyes sparkling with excitement. "The boulder has been moved and the tunnel is open! Shall we go in?" "Oh my goodness. This is so exciting! Did you bring the head torches?"

"Of course!" Harry was already putting his on. He passed her the bag.

"Okay, let's make sure the coast is clear," said Annabelle. "We have to be really quiet. Milly – that means you too."

Milly wagged her tail so fast Annabelle thought it might fall off. The children crept towards the entrance of the tunnel. Just like the other day there were prints from flippers in the sand right up to the entrance.

"Look at the prints. You can see where the boulder has been pushed aside too," whispered Annabelle, pointing at the marks in the sand. There was just enough of a gap for them to squeeze through. The children used their head torches to see what it was like inside. At the entrance was a wide cavern.

It smelt of the sea and was littered with sand
and seaweed. Towards the back of the cavern the
children could see it got much narrower and was
more like a tunnel. Although, as they had read in
Elise's diary, there was still space for a horse to get
through. It was very dark apart from at the entrance:
the sunlight flooded in where the boulder had been
moved aside. The floor of the cavern was sandy,
leading to a rocky floor.

"Look, Annabelle. The prints from the flippers continue inside!" whispered Harry as he pointed to the floor. Annabelle's heart was beating furiously in case whoever had made the prints came back. Silently the children followed the prints to a rock. Milly sniffed each print.

"Oh my goodness!" said Annabelle. Harry spotted them too.

"Someone's been diving! There are two sets of oxygen tanks, mouthpieces, flippers and diving masks. Wow! Look at this bit of wetsuit on the rock. It looks like whoever walked past the rock got caught against it and this ripped off."

They could see footprints leading off towards the tunnel at the back of the cavern and then disappearing as the floor turned to rock.

Suddenly the children heard voices. Milly growled. They looked desperately for somewhere to hide. Luckily the rock where they had found the diving equipment was big and the children could tuck themselves behind it without being seen. Annabelle shook Harry and pointed at his head torch. Harry managed to switch it off just in time. The last thing Annabelle saw before it went dark was Harry's frightened eyes. She held his hand to reassure him and he grabbed it tightly. She was sure he must be able to hear her heart. It was beating loudly in her chest as whoever made the prints got nearer. She held Milly's collar tightly with her other hand. She couldn't imagine what would happen if Milly ran out and gave their hiding position away.

"Well, why did you drop it, you idiot?" said a man's voice.

Another man's voice replied, "I didn't do it on purpose. I thought I had it! Mrs Wilson from the beach cafe reckons those kids have taken it to the museum. There's no way we can get it back now!"

"He's going to be furious!" said the first man's voice. "We're in so much trouble and those kids are to blame."

Harry squeezed Annabelle's hand even tighter as they both realised the men were talking about them. Annabelle put an arm round him and reassured Milly to stop her barking.

"Just a few more days and we can get the rest of the jewels and those coins. We haven't found everything that was on the list yet, remember. There'll be something in that lot to keep him happy. He wouldn't have found the wreck without us. Come on we've got to get back to work or we'll be missed."

They could hear the sound of the men running, then the boulder being pushed back into place.

The sunlight that had rushed in from the entrance suddenly disappeared and the cavern they were hiding in was plunged into darkness.

"We're trapped, Annabelle," said Harry, his voice shaking. "How are we going to get out?"

Annabelle tried to remain calm. But she had no idea. How were they going to escape?

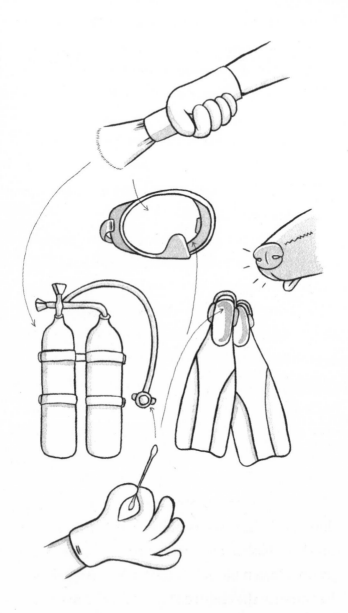

Chapter 7
Trapped in the dark

(T)here must be a way out. Annabelle felt scared but determined.

"Harry, I think the men have gone now. Switch on your head torch. Let's look for a way to escape. There'll be one."

She thought if she sounded positive Harry wouldn't worry. She could see, now her head torch was on, that he was trying to be brave.

"Let's see if we can push the boulder, Harry," she suggested. She already knew it would be too heavy from when they had tried the other day on the beach.

"It's no good. Maybe we could try moving it using our legs?" said Harry.

Milly barked encouragement at the children. The boulder, however, remained where it was. Annabelle flashed her torch around the walls of the cavern. When it hit the tunnel leading away from the entrance she realised the answer had been there all along!

"Of course! Harry – according to the book from the library and Elise's diary the tunnel leads to the church. We just need to follow this tunnel and we can escape from there!"

Harry hugged Annabelle. He felt so relieved. He hadn't meant to show Annabelle he was so scared. It was obvious, though!

"Who do you think those men were, Annabelle? They're stealing Elise's mum's jewels and the gold coins from the shipwreck. I think they're diving down for them." He pointed at the diving equipment. "They must've dropped the locket by mistake when they were bringing it back to the tunnel and now whoever else is involved is cross with them."

"I agree. Do you remember the book we have from the library? It has a list of the jewels in it that were onboard. So whoever read the book before us would've known about the list and they would know about the smuggler's tunnel. Remember – the men in the library said it was a really popular book."

"Annabelle, everyone in Tresorporth seems to know about the smuggler's tunnel. They just don't know where the entrances are. But that's true about the list – and do you remember the book was covered in dirty fingerprints? I bet the diving masks are too. If we can match the fingerprints we could work out who is stealing the jewels and coins!"

"Harry, you're forgetting we can also use DNA! Whoever wore the mouthpieces, diving masks and flippers would've left their DNA all over it. Remember anything living will have DNA including humans and everyone's DNA is unique. If we can match the DNA from the diving equipment with a suspect we'll definitely know who it is!" A shiver of excitement went through Annabelle, and she went on. "Harry – you realise this is a case for the 'DNA Detectives'. We can solve this mystery and find out who is stealing the treasure!"

She wished she had her notebook so she could write this down. She'd do that later. She looked at Harry, but instead of looking excited and ready to solve the mystery he looked confused and scratched his head.

"I can't remember why the men's DNA would be on the diving stuff. I know we learnt about it in Mum's forensic science workshop where we used DNA to solve a crime. Can you remind me?"

"Not now, Harry. We need to get out of here in case those men come back. I'll tell you later, I promise. Quickly, let's take some samples. It was a good job you brought our 'DNA Detectives' kit.

Remember, wherever the skin would have made contact with the items we can get DNA."

"I do remember that!" said Harry. "And we need to wear gloves and facemasks to stop the samples being contaminated with our own DNA." He passed some gloves to Annabelle and a facemask. "Shouldn't we wear overalls too?"

"We should really, Harry, but I want to get out of here. We'll just have to chance it."

Harry took the cotton buds out of his bag and they quickly took samples from each item. Milly tried to help by sniffing the diving gear.

"Keep off, Milly. We are trying to collect DNA." Harry pulled her away and Milly's tail disappeared between her legs. She felt sad to not be involved.

"Tell me where the DNA would be," said Annabelle smiling.

"On the mouthpiece, where the person's mouth would be. For the diving mask where it rubs against their face and for the flippers inside here where their feet would rub against the plastic."

"Very good, Harry. I'll label the bags so we know which sample comes from which equipment. Let's put that bit of ripped wetsuit into a bag too. Maybe if we can find someone with a ripped wetsuit that would give us a clue. The masks look dry. Can you dust the mask with cocoa powder to see if we can get some fingerprints? Use Mum's make-up brush to help. I'll do the other mask."

"I have fingerprints, Annabelle!"

"Great! Use the sellotape to peel them off and stick them to the white card so we can see them. We need to hurry!"

"I wonder who the men are?"

"From their accent they are local and they sound young," said Annabelle, as she quickly put the samples into the bag.

"They must work near here as they said they had to get back to work before they were missed," said Harry, his mind whirring with ideas as to who the mystery young men could be. They had already met several men from Tresorporth that fitted that description.

"Come on, Harry. We've got all the evidence. It's time to get out of here. Follow me!" Annabelle ran as fast as she could towards the tunnel at the back of the cavern. She used her head torch to light the path so she didn't fall in the darkness. Milly barked, sniffed the ground and followed behind her, with her tail wagging as fast as it could. Harry was surprised at how fast Annabelle was running; he had really wanted to be ahead, but he loyally followed her through the tunnel, trusting that she would find the way out for them.

The tunnel twisted through the rock, sometimes dipping down, and then gradually started going uphill. The walls of the tunnel were damp and the salty smell at the entrance was replaced by a musty, mouldy odour. The children could hear water dripping through the crevices and, at points where the water collected, the ground was muddy. Eventually, as Elise had described in her diary, they arrived at an old wooden door.

"Annabelle, try and open it!" said Harry.

Very slowly Annabelle pushed the door. There was something against it, making it hard to open. As the door gradually opened the children could see there was a large tapestry hung over it.

"That must be to hide the entrance," whispered Harry.

He stuck his head out and looked around. "Quick, Annabelle. I think the coast is clear,"

Annabelle followed Harry out of the door. Both children looked up. "Look – you can see the bell up there in the tower! Just like Elise described it. I think we can get out of this door." Harry pushed open the only other door in the room. They were in such a hurry to get out and get back to the beach they knocked into a table.

"Annabelle! Look what you did!"

"It wasn't me. What did *you* knock over?"

"It looks like the visitors' book. Quick – put it back and let's go!"

The children ran as fast as they could through the church to the main doors.

"Wait, Harry! There's someone there." Annabelle held her arm out to stop Harry running out and giving them away. She grabbed Milly with her other arm.

"It's a lady. She looks very old. It's okay... I don't think *she's* involved with the thieves! It looks like she's putting flowers on that grave over there. The one that looks out to sea. She won't see us if we sneak out. Let's go or we'll be late for the surf lesson." Both children ran as fast as they could with Milly out of the church grounds and down the road towards the beach.

✳ ✳ ✳

"There you are, you two!" shouted Mum. "Meet my friend Paula, this is Josh, he's nine years old – like you, Harry – and this is Ellie, she's 11 years old just like you, Annabelle. If you follow them they will take you into the surf centre and show you where you can change into these wet suits. Go quickly, I think the lesson is about to start! Give Milly to me. She's not surfing today!"

Annabelle smiled at Ellie. She reminded her of her friend Issy from home, with her brown hair and freckles on her nose. She was tall like Issy, too.

"Follow me!" said Ellie. Harry was already talking with Josh about football. Annabelle knew they were going to become good friends!

"Here you go – the changing rooms. We've got our wetsuits on already so we'll see you outside!" Ellie and Josh waved and headed outside. Annabelle was about to enter her changing room when she noticed something. She prodded Harry excitedly.

"What?" Harry said, angrily. He didn't like being prodded. She pointed at a wetsuit which was hanging over the changing room door. It had a tear in it.

"Harry, grab that bit of ripped wetsuit. I'll see if it matches." Just like a jigsaw the piece of ripped wetsuit fitted into the hole perfectly.

"That means one of the men who was in the smuggler's tunnel was here in the Surf Centre!" said Annabelle, feeling delighted. They were a step closer to finding the thief.

"Well, it could still be anyone. Everyone in Tresorporth seems to surf!" said Harry. "I saw loads

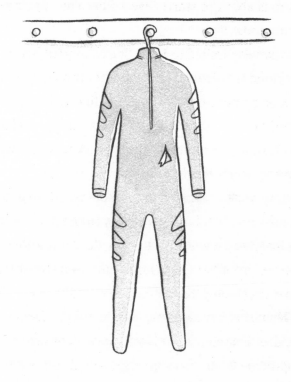

of people out there this morning when I looked out of the window."

Annabelle looked disappointed.

As she and Harry headed to the beach for their surf lesson, they saw two men talking to the vicar.

"Who are they? Goodness, the vicar looks really cross!" said Harry.

"Do you know who those men are?" said

Annabelle to Ellie. Maybe they were the men from the smuggler's tunnel.

"That's Alex and Peter, the twins," replied Ellie. "They're the instructors for the surf school. They'll be taking the lesson today. They're so funny. You'll love them!"

Maybe not, thought Annabelle. They sounded like they were really nice.

"Is the vicar cross with everyone?" asked Annabelle.

"Yes! Everyone. He's so grumpy. I don't know why he wanted to be a vicar. You really don't want to get on the wrong side of him. I think the twins must've done something dreadful!"

"He doesn't like us at all," said Harry "He keeps giving us horrid looks and we haven't done anything."

"That's normal," laughed Josh. "There are rumours that his great-great-grandfather from a long time ago was also a vicar and used to help the smugglers to hide their stolen goods in the church!"

Annabelle and Harry looked at each other.

"Maybe the vicar Josh is describing is the same vicar Elise talks about in her diary," whispered Annabelle to Harry. He nodded in agreement. The children watched as the vicar walked off crossly, shouted something at the lifeguards and then stormed off up the hill to the church.

"Sorry about that! We'll be taking the surf lesson today," said one of the twins. It was very difficult to tell them apart as they looked exactly the same.

The other twin said, "I don't recognise you two. Are you on holiday?"

"We are!" said Harry bravely.

"Hold on. Aren't you the children who found the locket? That is amazing. Is that right you gave it to the museum? Will you get it back?"

"I hope so," said Harry "I think it's really valuable."

Goodness, thought Annabelle – someone else who knew about the locket. So far there were the men from the library, the bakery, the lifeguards and now the surf instructors. It was interesting that they were all young, had local accents, worked here in the cove and all seemed very interested in the locket. Did they all use the surf club? If so, that meant they were all suspects.

Annabelle's brain couldn't stop thinking about the evidence they had got as the twins explained how to stand up on the surfboard. They'd already established that whoever had the book before them could have used it to find out what treasure was on the wreck. They'd left grubby fingerprints all over the page. They also had DNA from the diving gear. That reminded her she must remember to explain to

Harry why there was DNA on the diving equipment. All they needed now was DNA and fingerprints from the suspects. If they could find a match from the suspects to the fingerprints and DNA they already had, they could find out who was stealing treasure from the shipwreck.

But how were they going to get fingerprints and DNA from the suspects? This really was a challenge for the "DNA Detectives" and maybe there were more clues to help them in the diary. Annabelle wished the surf lesson could be over so that she and Harry could come up with a plan. She looked around. The others were heading for the sea with their surfboards. It looked like she would have to wait.

Chapter 8
The Suspects

"See you later!" shouted Annabelle and Harry to their new friends, waving furiously as Josh and Ellie disappeared up the hill with Paula.

"Thanks for inviting them over," said Annabelle to Mum. "They're such good fun. I loved the surfing too and my surfboard. Alex said it's called a 'boogie board'. It's smaller than the other surfboards and you have to lie on it. They're the best! Come here, Milly – did you miss us?" Milly came over, gave Annabelle a sniff and then licked her face.

"You must be really dirty," laughed Mum. "Harry, are you okay now?"

"I'm fine, thanks. I meant to do that!" said Harry, defensively. He had insisted on having a proper surfboard and had stepped too far forward, overbalanced and fallen off. A wave had caught him and tumbled him over. He had finally got to the surface coughing and spluttering and everyone had laughed. He looked really cross.

"Not to worry, here's Dad with some lunch. Hot sausage rolls and doughnuts – your favourite!"

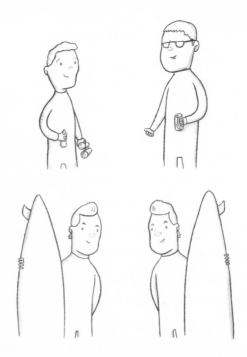

Mum gave Harry a cuddle to cheer him up.

"Mum! Don't! I'm too old for that now!" said Harry. "Someone might see!"

Sensing Harry's unhappiness, Annabelle grabbed his arm in one hand and their lunch in the other.

"We'll see you later. We're off to look in the rock pools!" she shouted as she dragged Harry away. Milly ran after them, knowing they couldn't refuse her "hungry" look. Soon she would have a tummy full of hot sausage rolls and doughnuts. The older humans weren't so good at falling for her trick!

"Thanks for helping me escape being cuddled!" said

Harry smiling as he got a huge sausage roll out of the bag. It was still warm – his favourite!

"We need a plan to get DNA and fingerprints from our suspects," Annabelle said. "Is my notepad in your bag?"

"Of course."

Annabelle grabbed the bag and rummaged round till she found her notepad. "Okay. Who are our suspects?"

"The men at the library, definitely. The men from the bakery, the lifeguards and of course the twins from the surf club. I can't think of anyone else." Eating and thinking was difficult for Harry!

"Hold on," he said, still with his mouth full. "What about the vicar? He always seems cross when we see him. I think he's acting really suspiciously and Josh told us his great-great-grandfather was involved with smugglers."

"That doesn't mean he is! Everyone says he's just grumpy. Anyway, it can't have been him in the smuggler's tunnel. He's really old. The men we heard were young." Annabelle broke off a bit of her sausage roll and gave it to Milly.

"Good point. We need to get DNA and fingerprints from all of them, don't we?" said Harry.

Annabelle wrote the list of suspects in her notepad. She wrote "DNA and fingerprints" in a column next to the names.

"What about the samples we need from the smuggler's tunnel, to compare them with?" she said, with pen at the ready. "Remind me of what we have, Harry."

"Okay!" As Harry listed them he counted on his fingers. "We need to collect fingerprints from the library book and we have DNA from the mouthpieces, diving masks and flippers. Can you please tell me now why people's DNA gets left behind?"

"Okay, but stop chomping in my face and making mouth noises." Harry made a face at Annabelle, but he moved back. She thought about Mum's forensic science workshop and how to explain it to Harry like Mum had. "You know your Lego model kit to make a Star Wars Droid Microfighter? Well, to build it you needed the instructions and that's what DNA is, the instructions to make a human. Our own set of building instructions. The Lego is kept in a box to stop it getting damaged and our DNA is kept in a special bag to stop it getting damaged. That bag is called a cell. Cells are all over our bodies on the inside and the outside. In fact there are 37 trillion cells in our entire bodies!"

"No way!" gasped Harry.

"If you imagine the number 37 trillion in seconds then that would be the equivalent of 1,167,202 years. Which is a lot! Cells are so tiny you can only see them with a microscope."

"That's amazing!"

"I know. I learnt it from Mum," agreed Annabelle. "Our skin is made up of these cells all containing DNA. When we touch something some of our cells brush off. Because our DNA is in our cells we will leave our DNA behind. The same thing happens with our hair, dandruff, wee, poo, blood, bogies and saliva. They're all made of cells all full of DNA."

"Well I'm glad the thieves didn't leave poo or bogies behind! That's disgusting!"

"I know, but we're all walking sources of DNA and everyone's DNA is different."

"Apart from identical twins! Their DNA is the same but not their fingerprints," said Harry proudly, delighted he had remembered that. "So the thieves have left their skin cells in the mouthpieces, diving masks and the flippers. So we should get lots of DNA."

"Correct! They may also have left saliva in the mouthpiece which will be full of cells from their cheeks. A great source of DNA."

"So we just need to work out a plan to collect DNA from our suspects," said Harry, thinking and biting into his doughnut. Milly thought he was sharing and went to take some too. "Get off, that's mine!" he laughed.

"Well we know what things are sources of DNA and fingerprints now so we need to collect things like that from the suspects like items of clothing, something they have drunk out of, tissues. Basically anything they touch! Maybe you could create a distraction, Harry!"

"I'm brilliant at that, of course! Didn't we get in trouble for taking samples of DNA without asking last time?" asked Harry, not wanting to get in trouble again. They had the iPad taken away from them before and he had a fantastic new football game on it. He wasn't sure he wanted to risk losing that!

"Well we did... But this is an emergency. These men

are stealing Elise's mum's jewellery. It needs to be returned to her family. We've got to do this for Elise. Thing is, we haven't got Mum's laboratory like we had before to get the DNA."

A vision of Mum's laboratory in their garden at home flashed up in Annabelle's mind. It made her feel happy. She loved being in there helping Mum with her samples. She and Harry even had their own lab coats. This was a tricky one – how were they going to get the DNA analysed?

"I've got it!" said Annabelle, jumping up, almost tipping her doughnut out of the bag into a rock pool. She rescued it just in time. "Mum's collecting samples from local people for her study. Do you remember she's looking at people's DNA to see whether people whose families originally come from Cornwall are Celtic, Anglo-Saxon, or something else. Josh and Ellie are Cornish and their families have lived in Cornwall for a long time. Why don't we pretend to take samples from Josh, Ellie and their mum but replace them with our samples? We could ask Josh and Ellie if they've got some other Cornish friends and get samples from them too. That way we would cover all the samples we plan to take and Mum would never know! I've seen the results Mum gets from the samples she's taken already. It's a pattern. We just need to see if the pattern of

DNA from the diving gear matches that of some of the suspects and we'll know who the thieves are!"

Harry did a funny dance, which made Annabelle laugh. Milly jumped up and joined in too.

"We did it!" Harry shouted in delight.

"Well," thought Annabelle, "*I* did it!", but then she remembered how sad he had looked earlier when everyone had laughed at him, and so decided not to say anything.

✳ ✳ ✳

The plan worked like a dream! Josh, Ellie and Paula had all been very excited about taking part in Mum's study. Annabelle and Harry had spent the afternoon helping Mum collect samples from them all. They had used a cotton bud to rub inside their cheeks and then placed all the buds into a special tube. Mum had made them fill in a form to say they were happy for the samples to be taken.

"Of course, the cells in the cheek are an excellent source of DNA!" said Harry loudly so everyone could hear. Annabelle was impressed at how much he had remembered from their discussion on the beach earlier. She could tell Mum was really proud of him

too. They visited various friends and neighbours of Josh and Ellie who were all Cornish and wanted samples taken when word had spread about Mum's study. It seemed everyone wanted to know if they were originally Celtic or Anglo-Saxon!

"Look, Harry," said Annabelle while they were having tea. She pointed to the collection of samples in the kitchen.

"Thanks for your help collecting these," said Mum "I won't need many more now to complete the study.

I'm going to send them off to the university to be analysed tomorrow afternoon. We should have the initial results by Thursday."

That didn't give them long to substitute the samples, thought Annabelle. They were going to have to be quick and go and collect them from the suspects first thing the next morning. But before that, they were going to read some more of Elise's diary before bed. What other clues were there to be found? Annabelle couldn't wait. She caught Harry's eye. He was obviously thinking the same thing. She almost jumped off her chair with the jolt of excitement that went through her. "Come on bedtime – hurry up!" she thought.

Chapter 9
The Smuggler's tunnel

"G et the diary, Annabelle!" whispered Harry as they ran upstairs. They had insisted on reading by themselves again and Mum and Dad seemed pleased they could sit downstairs and relax. Annabelle put her hand under her pillow and was relieved to feel the leather front cover of the diary.

She opened the page to where they had finished reading the previous night, and resumed:

"*Sunday, March 20th, 1881.*

I know the men are plotting something. Henry has had different visitors at all times throughout the day. Each time I've heard heated discussions behind closed doors. I heard them in the bar this evening when I was mopping the floor before I went to bed. They're making plans for tonight. A message has come that there are several ships making their way along the coastline and I feel a storm is brewing. Tonight I will follow them and find out what they're up to.

I heard the crunch of the bar stools on the floor
and the noise of the men got louder as they prepared
to leave. I dressed quickly so I could follow them.
As I pulled on my tights I caught sight of my foot.
I must not let the family see it, for on my left foot
I've got six toes! I know if they see it they will think
me the devil. I was born with six toes just like my
mother and my granny who had the same. To us it's
normal. But this family, I believe, would see it as a
curse. I must remember to keep my feet covered at
all times. If I'm thrown out I'll have nowhere to go
and then what will become of me?

I crept down the stairs, silently and unheard. I knew which steps creaked and were best avoided. The voices were coming from the kitchen. I waited in the darkness of the corridor till it had all gone quiet. Slowly I turned the handle of the kitchen door but no one was there. It was so quiet I knew they must all be in the tunnel by now. I watched them go into it before but until now I hadn't been brave enough to follow them. I needed answers, though. I need to know how they were able to lure my father's ship onto the rocks. I reached inside the fireplace and to the left. Inside was a small gap in the stone where I knew they kept another spare key."

Annabelle stopped reading and turned to Harry.

"Harry, there's a second tunnel. I don't think anyone knows about this tunnel! It's not mentioned in any of the books. People only talk about the tunnel from the beach to the church. The only fireplace in the cottage is in the lounge. Maybe the lounge used to be the kitchen!"

"That would make sense! I can't wait to have a look. Keep reading, Annabelle – I want to hear more about the tunnel!" Harry was literally on the edge of his seat!

Annabelle carried on reading:

"I carefully went to the panelled wall on the left of the fire and removed the bottom panel, just as I'd seen the men do since I had been here. Grabbing a candle from the mantelpiece I stepped into the gap and replaced the panel so I didn't give the game away. I crept slowly and carefully down the spiral staircase behind the fire. The steps were worn and uneven from years of use. This staircase must hold many stories!

I'd only seen as far as the spiral stairs before. I assumed there must be a door at the bottom because of the key. Sure enough I found it at the bottom of the stairs. It was an old wooden door. I unlocked it with the key and put the key into my pocket. As it opened I could hear the men ahead. Their voices echoed along the walls of the tunnel. I knew they wouldn't be coming back this way. At least not yet – there was work to be done! I ran down the tunnel after the men as quietly as possible. Luckily my cloak was black so I could blend into the darkness and I knew I could quickly blow out the candle if I needed to.

I checked the key was safe in my pocket and touched my penny for luck. It was the penny my father gave me which kept me safe that fateful day when The Helena sunk. I hoped it would keep me safe tonight. As I followed the men through the tunnel it met with a second tunnel. I'm sure this was the tunnel I was taken through that night I was rescued from The Helena.

I think that tunnel runs from the beach to the church. I looked back at the tunnel I'd come from and realised it was impossible to see if you were coming from the beach. The tunnel to the inn was set back and around the corner from the second tunnel. Unless you knew it was there you wouldn't see it. I had to remember how to find the tunnel I'd just come from. I realised the second tunnel to the church forked sharply to the left at this point. I needed to remember that, so I could find my way back. As I got to the end nearest the beach the tunnel started to open out into a cavern. The smell changed from a musty smell to the salty smell of the ocean. It was still cold and damp however. The wind was wild and whipped around a boulder that blocked the entrance to the tunnel. The storm was reaching its peak. The men had stopped. In the light of their lanterns I could see Henry Nance standing beside the boulder. Two men were pushing it aside to reveal an opening to the beach. The wind came howling in. They had reached the beach. Henry stood in the entrance and held a telescope to his eye.

He was looking out to sea.

"Ship ahoy! Take this lantern put it on the rock. It's time friends!" He rubbed his hands together in glee. Two men ran forward with a funny-shaped lantern. There was a spout at the front and the light from it was cast forward only and not to the sides."

"It's a Spout Lantern, Annabelle," said Harry. "Like the one we saw at the museum."

"I think you're right," agreed Annabelle. "Hold on – something has happened."

She resumed reading from the diary:

"I watched the men run down the beach and hide behind rocks. I crept to the entrance to follow them. As I did, the wind caught my candle and blew it out. It was useless now so I threw it to the ground. I looked out to sea and saw the ship turn and head towards the beach. I could see the lantern the men had placed up on the rocks. It was so bright. The ship just like The Helena *– must've thought they'd found a safe harbour where they could shelter from the storm.*

I wanted to shout to warn them but they wouldn't be able to hear me above the sound of the wind and the waves. What could I do? But it was too late – the ship hit the rocks under the water and started to roll onto its side. The men on the beach launched their smaller boats into the water under the guidance of Henry. They were quickly aboard the sinking ship and I saw them load their goods into the boats. The men were soon rowing back to the shore.

I ran back to the tunnel before they realised I was watching them. It was then that I heard a shout and a gunshot ring out from the cliffs. To my horror I looked up at the cliffs above the beach and saw they were filled with men. From their dress I could see the men were customs officers. It would appear Henry had been rumbled and they were here to arrest the gang.

The men on the beach were alerted by the noise and ran up the beach carrying the goods with them towards the tunnel as the customs officers descended from the cliffs. The sound and smell of gunfire filled my lungs. I was terrified. I ran back into the tunnel but without my candle it was hard to see where I was going. There were small shafts of light at the entrance of the tunnel shining in where the sun was just starting to rise across the beach. I could just about see as I ran as fast as I could to the back of the cavern. Here the tunnel narrowed and the light disappeared.

It was now completely dark. As Henry's men shouted and ran into the entrance I used my hands to feel along the wall. The rock was sharp but suddenly disappeared inwards. There was a small opening. I managed to creep into the narrow opening in the rock and hide out of sight. I hid away crouched in the darkness, hardly daring to breathe. I heard the pounding of feet as the men struggled with their stolen goods through the tunnel. The light from their lanterns flickered against the walls. The men were out of breath. I could hear the fear in their voices. Next were the customs officers. They were not far behind the men. They were moving so fast. I was sure the men would be caught and then what? I knew the penalties were harsh. Even though Henry frightened me he had taken me into his home. I didn't want him to be caught but there was nothing I could do.

I waited for what felt like a long time crouched on the floor. I was just about to leave the safety of my hiding place in the rock when I could hear footsteps and voices again.

'Where are they? We got to the church but there was no sign of them.''Tell me they haven't got away. But there was nowhere for them to go. Let's search the graveyard again. Come on follow me. They must

be caught!' Incredibly it seemed like Henry and the gang had got away. Of course I realised they must have escaped up the secret tunnel back to the Inn. If you didn't know where it was there was no way you would find it. Now the customs officers were gone I needed to get out of the tunnel. I was too scared to follow the tunnel back to the Inn. I decided my best bet was to head for the beach. The ship must have sunk fast – there was no sign of it as I headed back up the path from the beach to the village.

I managed to sneak into the inn without being seen. The men were long gone. I crept into my bed hoping that nobody had checked on me and realised I was missing. I felt into my pocket. They key was still there but not my lucky penny. I pushed my hand right to the bottom.

No luck – I must've lost it when I was hiding in the opening in the rock. Was that it? Had my luck run out? I didn't dare return the key. If I got caught Henry might think it was me that told the customs officers he was planning to wreck the ship that night. I knew there was a loose floorboard underneath the window. I pulled it up and hid the key inside.

I woke to hear Henry whistling. He seemed to me to be particularly cheerful. I looked at the window and saw the little statue was facing outwards. It was

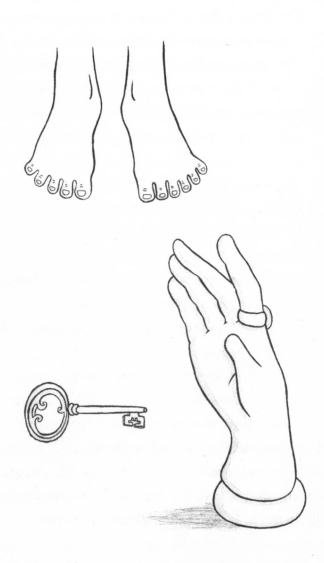

a statue of a hand with a ring on one of the fingers.
If the palm of the hand was facing the window it
meant there was nothing to offer 'an empty hand'.
If the ring faced the window it meant 'ring at
the door – there are goods on hand'. It was quite
incredible – not only had Henry and his men escaped
being arrested; they'd also got away with the goods!"

"Oh my goodness, what a story!" said Harry.
"A second tunnel! I wonder if the key is still there
under the floorboards."

"Maybe if we can find the second tunnel, and
the opening in the rock where Elise hid, we might
find her lucky penny. That would be incredible!"
said Annabelle, immediately thinking of all the
possibilities.

"Let's have a look!" said Harry, already heading
over to the window. Annabelle closed her eyes – she
didn't even dare to believe that the key would still be
there after all these years. Harry stuck a pen in a gap
between the floorboards under the window. Magically,
the floorboard was loose and Harry was able to slowly
lift it up. He peered inside! Would it be there?

Chapter 10
Under the floor boards

"I t's not there, Annabelle. I can't see a key!"
Harry sounded deflated. He really thought
it would be there.

"Move out of the way. Let me see."

Annabelle knew Harry would have done his
"Harry style" of looking, which involved a quick
look, assume it's not there and then shout for
Mum. Annabelle reached her hand into the gap
beneath the floorboard and felt around. It was only
when her hand reached the furthest point that she
touched something which felt like metal and was
about the right size for a key. She quickly grabbed
hold of it, dragged it towards her, out of the hole
in the floor boards and up into the light of the
bedroom. As she did, she crossed her fingers – it
was what she thought it was.

"It's the key! You found it!" Harry hugged
Annabelle with excitement. "I wonder why I didn't
find it?" he said, looking surprised.

Annabelle rolled her eyes! Then she said,

"I can't believe we have the key! This is so exciting. Now we've got the key I think we should try and find the second tunnel. We might even find Elise's lucky penny."

"Great idea!" said Harry, already heading out of the room. As he went, Annabelle grabbed him by the hood of his top.

"We can't go yet, Mum and Dad are in the lounge. Besides we need to get DNA and fingerprints from our suspects today so we can substitute the samples before Mum sends them away. I'll put the key in this drawer so we know it's safe. We'll need it later!"

"Good idea. I totally forgot about the samples. I'm just so excited about the tunnel!"

"Really, Harry, I would never have guessed!" said Annabelle, laughing. "Help me check everything's in the bag which we need for collecting fingerprints and DNA. Put it on the bed when I read it out so we can make sure it's there." Harry nodded and grabbed the bag. "Overalls, gloves, facemasks, plastic sandwich bags to put the samples in, a pen to write on the bag, cotton buds, scissors, sellotape, cocoa powder, white card, wet wipes and Mum's make up brush."

"Check! All there. We can't wear overalls or facemasks though or people will know we're up to something!"

"Oh yes! I forgot about that. We'll just have to wear gloves and be really careful we don't contaminate the samples. We already have the book from the library. We'll get the fingerprints from that when we get back. Harry, can you persuade Mum to take us to the library?"

"Easy! Watch this," said Harry, strutting off into the kitchen where Mum was getting breakfast ready. Annabelle knew that in a short while they would be heading off to the library. This was an easy challenge for Harry!

✳✳✳

Luckily when they arrived the library was quiet. As the electric doors of the library whooshed open Harry spotted one of the men. "Look, Annabelle – the man with the glasses and freckles is over there on the computer. Let's go and watch him. We can see what he's touching and decide what samples to take! Follow me!"

Annabelle followed Harry to a shelf that was

just behind the computer desk where the man was sitting working. They peered in between the shelves so they could see what he was doing. Mum had gone off to find a book to read about local history.

"Look, he's touching the screen with his finger. I bet he's left a fingerprint on it! And he's chewing a pen. We need that pen! Harry, can you cause a distraction?"

"Of course I can. I'm a pro! Watch this!" Harry walked over to the desk and said something to the man. The man then obediently followed Harry to the far end of the library.

"This is my chance," thought Annabelle, checking no one was around and quickly putting on a pair of gloves. She carefully picked up the pen, holding it by the end which hadn't been in the man's mouth, and put it into a bag. She labelled it with "library man 1 glasses".

Next, just like Mum had shown them in her fingerprint workshop and like they had done in the tunnel, she tipped some cocoa powder into a bag and dipped the make-up brush into it. It was tricky to get the powder onto the surface of the computer screen. She had noted when she was watching the man that he had touched the bottom left corner. Sure enough a beautiful fingerprint emerged highlighted by the cocoa. She checked no one was about and cut a piece of sellotape. Carefully she placed the sellotape over the print. As she slowly peeled the sellotape away, she could see the fingerprint had transferred from the computer screen onto the sellotape. She stuck the sellotape onto a piece of white card so they would be able to study it later and then placed it into a labelled bag. Using a wet wipe she cleared away any traces of cocoa from the desk and computer. No one would know she had been there. Now to find Harry to tell him she had got the fingerprints.

It was then that she spotted the second man. The one with ginger hair. He was pushing books on a shelf so they could be returned. He saw Annabelle and waved. She waved back. Where was Harry? Then she spotted him in the children's section.

"There you are!" Harry looked up and smiled at her. He was surrounded by a pile of books and the man was searching for something for him.

"What's he looking for?" whispered Annabelle, amused to find out what excuse Harry had come up with.

"I said I was looking for a Roald Dahl book but I couldn't remember which one. They've got loads!"

Annabelle smiled. Then he shouted, "Hold on!", holding up a copy of *Esio Trot* from the pile.
"I think it's this one!"

"Glad you found it," said the man. "Let me know if there's anything else I can do to help. Have you got your locket back yet?"

Annabelle and Harry looked at each other.

"Not yet," said Annabelle pulling Harry away.

"I've found the second man. He's over there putting books away. I think his fingerprints will be on the shelf he's pushing. Can you distract him?"

Harry ran over to the man. Annabelle watched as the man followed him to another shelf, some distance from where the man was working. She watched as both of them crouched on the floor and appeared to be looking for something. She checked the coast was clear then quickly brushed some cocoa powder over the surface of the shelf where the man had been pushing it. There were some beautiful prints. She quickly used the tape to collect them and then put them in a bag. She labelled it "library man 2 ginger hair". Then she went to find Harry. She could see his big grin from across the library.

"I know how we can get DNA from the man!" Harry looked extremely pleased with himself. "I got him to help me look for my Lego man. We looked under the shelf and the dust made him sneeze. He blew his nose and threw the tissue in the bin over there. Lots of bogies and DNA on that tissue – it was a big sneeze!"

"Ughhh! That's disgusting. But well done, Harry. Trust you to remember bogies are a great source of DNA. That's because they're full of cells from your nose." Annabelle was glad she had her gloves on when she retrieved the tissue from the bin and put it in a labelled bag. Maybe bogies weren't so bad when she considered some of the other disgusting samples from your body that you could get DNA from.

"Next stop, home to get Milly," shouted Harry, "then the bakery, and we've got a lesson at the surf club this afternoon so we can get samples from Alex and Peter the surf instructors and the lifeguards Adam and Billy on the way. Let's get Mum and go to the bakery." Then he ran off.

✻✻✻

The bell on top of the door rang as the children entered the bakery. Mum waved at them from outside where she stood looking after Milly. The little dog was delighted they were going to her new favourite shop. Her tail wagged and her eyes sparkled. She licked her lips in anticipation. Little did she know that Annabelle and Harry were under strict orders from Mum to buy four pasties and four doughnuts... and nothing for Milly!

"Hello, my lovelies! How are you this fine morning? Any sign of getting that lovely locket back?" Annabelle noticed both men had a pair of tongs in their hands ready to serve them. Interestingly they were standing in the same position behind the counter as they had been the other day. Maybe the taller of the men was always on the left and the one with the blond hair was always on the right?

"We're fine, thanks. Not yet. Do you have anything fresh out of the oven?" asked Annabelle, knowing they would have to go out to the oven in the back of the shop.

"We've got sausage rolls, doughnuts and fresh rolls. I think I might have something in the fridge for your dog too!"

"That sounds perfect. Four sausage rolls and four doughnuts, please! I'm sure Milly would like a treat if you have one," said Harry.

"Come on mate – you can help me," said the man to his friend. "The shop's quiet and these two have a big order." They laughed and disappeared out to the back of the shop.

"Quick, Annabelle – there's no one else in the shop and look, Mum's busy chatting to that women. This is our chance!" Harry passed Annabelle some gloves and put his on as quickly as he could.

"Harry, you collect fingerprints from the left of the counter and use a cotton bud to rub the tongs which the man on the left hand side of the counter has been using, for DNA. Rub the bit where he's been holding them – I'll do the same on the right. The tall man is always on the left, the blond man on the right, so if we label the samples carefully we'll be able to tell them apart. Quick before they come back!"

The time seemed to go really quickly. Harry could feel his heart pounding. He was *sure* they would get caught. He had just finished rubbing the tongs with a cotton bud when he heard footsteps coming from the back of the shop. At the same time the bell from the door rang and the door flew open. Annabelle shot round from behind the counter, as did Harry.

"You look very guilty," said the vicar, staring at them both.

When the men returned with the food, he told them, "These two children were behind your counter. Up to no good, I think, by the look of them."

Harry tried to take his gloves off in his pocket. He could see that Annabelle had pulled her top over her hands to cover hers. He wondered if his face was as red as Annabelle's. He could feel his face burning at the thought of getting caught. If the men saw their gloves or searched his pockets they'd find the cotton buds and the card with the fingerprints on them. Then they would be in trouble.

"I was trying to steal the cakes," said Harry. "Annabelle was trying to stop me. I'm really sorry."

"Oh my love! Don't worry, a boy after my own heart," laughed one of the men.

The other man laughed too. "I would've done the same when I was your age. This is homemade Cornish cake after all. No harm done. Looks like you didn't get any after all that!" Harry looked anxiously at Mum outside, but the man said, "I won't tell her, don't worry. Just tell me when you get that locket back. I'd love to have a look at it."

Harry grabbed the bags of food and Annabelle handed over the money.

"Don't forget the sausage for your dog. Don't look so worried, my loves. No harm done! See you soon."

As the children left the shop they walked past the vicar. He looked so cross that they had got away with it. Why did he want to get them in trouble?

"That was close!" whispered Harry to Annabelle as they walked down to the beach, with Milly running along beside them sniffing at the bags.

Harry was delighted they had got away with it. "Did you get your samples? I did, but only just!"

"Same. Let's label up the bags when we get to the beach. It's not good to have them in our pockets. They'll get contaminated. I hated that feeling of nearly being caught. I was so worried!"

"I loved it!" lied Harry. "Come on, let's try and find the lifeguards Adam and Billy before we have our lunch."

"Look, there they are outside the lifeguard station. What great timing!" said Annabelle. She and Harry watched as Adam and Billy finished their drinks and threw them into the bin. When the lifeguards left, the children ran over. Milly ran with them and sniffed around the bin. She loved being part of the adventure. Annabelle checked that no one was looking. She saw that Mum and Dad were busy chatting to someone from the surf club.

"All clear! Can you get them out, Harry?" Annabelle didn't want to put her hand in the bin.

There were leftover fish and chips in there and she was sure she had seen a wasp. She wouldn't tell Harry though, he hated wasps. It was all because one summer there had been wasps on the pavement where some fruit had fallen. Mum had thought they would be okay if they all ran as fast as they could to get through them. But Harry had open sandals on and a wasp had crawled inside and stung him. After that, Harry was not a fan of wasps.

"Stand back and have the bags ready!" Harry put on another pair of gloves and put his hand into the bin. He looked to see where the drinks were.

"Adam had a can of coke I think and Billy had water," said Annabelle.

"Got them! Label the bags, Annabelle. We should be able to get DNA and fingerprints from them. Saliva is a good source of DNA, isn't it?"

"It is, Harry. I'm so pleased. That was easier than getting the samples in the bakery!"

"Says you!" said Harry, wiping ketchup and a melted ice lolly off his hands.

"Surf club next," they both said together and laughed. They looked across the beach where Mum was calling them for their surf lesson.

As Annabelle and Harry walked into the changing rooms they heard voices. "Isn't that Alex and

Peter?" said Harry. "They must be putting on their wetsuits."

"It is," whispered Annabelle. "Those are Alex's flip-flops. Let's get some DNA from them. Rub around where his toes would be, Harry. I bet loads of skin cells have rubbed off on there." She watched as Harry put on his gloves and swiftly rubbed around the bit of the flip-flop where Alex's toes would be.

"Rats! I left my sunglasses by the mirror. I'll get them in a minute. How many kids have we got today, Alex?" The men chatted away but already Annabelle had a cotton bud and was rubbing the sunglasses.

"This bit around where the nose goes is great for DNA," whispered Annabelle. "It's where your glasses rub when they slide down your nose and you push them up." Just at that moment the locks on the changing room doors opened. The children whipped around just in time to not get caught, and the men came out.

"Hey! It's Annabelle and Harry from yesterday. Are you two going to get your wetsuits on? I think you should maybe try a boogie board today, Harry! Much easier than standing on the board."

The children watched as the men put their hands on the mirror and brought their faces close to the glass to check their hair was perfect. Seeing the children watching them, the men laughed.

"Gotta look good for your lesson, kids! See you in the surf!"

As soon as the men had gone Annabelle turned to Harry. "You get Alex's fingerprint, I'll get Peter's. That was perfect. It's like they *knew* we needed samples from them. It was all too easy!"

✳✳✳

"That was the best surf lesson ever!" said Harry as they walked through the door of the cottage. "I love boogie boarding."

"Only because, this time, you didn't fall in and get caught in the waves."

"I'm probably the best surfer in Cornwall," bragged Harry.

"Before your head gets so big you can't fit upstairs," said Annabelle, "we need to sort out the samples and substitute them for Mum's and quickly; she's about to take her samples to the university. They all need to look like Mum's samples so she won't suspect anything. They need to be cotton swabs and in the tubes Mum uses. I'll grab the spare tubes Mum has put in the drawer in the kitchen and label them like she does. Harry, can you rub cotton buds on the pen and the bogie bit of the tissue which we collected from the men in the library to get their DNA? We already have DNA on cotton buds which we collected from the tongs used by the men in the bakery, the drinks bottles used by Adam and Billy and from the flip-flops and sunglasses worn by Alex and Peter. I'll just put them in the tubes to look like Mum's samples. We must make sure we know which sample is which. Don't forget the samples from the diving gear too. That's really important or we'll have nothing to compare the suspects DNA with! All Mum's samples have a number. I'll make a note of which samples are which in my notepad. Mum and Dad are in the garden setting up the barbeque for later so they won't see us."

"We need to take fingerprints from the book we got from the library too," said Harry.

"Oh yes. I forgot about that. Let's do that after we've sorted out the other samples. There are plenty of grubby fingerprints on the pages to choose from!"

Annabelle carefully sealed the last tube and put them all in the brown envelope that was on the side in the kitchen. They had worked so quickly but it was a big relief to get all the samples finished. Just then Mum walked into the kitchen.

"There you are. Annabelle, pass me those samples I'm off to the university. I won't be long. Why don't you two play in the garden till I get back?"

Annabelle passed her mum the samples. She was in such a good mood. Soon they would know if the DNA from the diving equipment they found in the smuggler's tunnel matched with that of any of their suspects.

"Do you want to play football?" asked Harry enthusiastically. Annabelle waited until Mum had walked out of the door.

"Harry, you realise with Mum at the university and Dad outside preparing the barbeque there's no one in the lounge. We could search for the second Smuggler's Tunnel!"

Annabelle laughed as Harry dropped the football and ran inside. He looked like he would literally explode with excitement! She wondered if there really would be a smuggler's tunnel behind the fireplace in the lounge. Well if there was, they now had the key to unlock the door at the bottom of the spiral staircase. She ran after Harry, desperate to see if they could find the panelled wall. Milly ran after the children. She didn't want to miss out on anything.

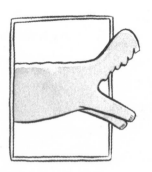

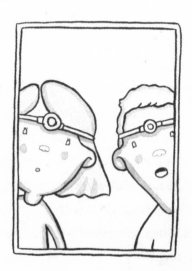

Chapter 11
The secret smugglers tunnel

"L" et's move this bench, Harry," said Annabelle. "Remember Elise said the panel is on the left side of the fireplace. I can't see any panelling. Shall we move this tapestry? Be careful!"

Harry jumped up on the bench and lifted up the tapestry. Milly started barking at him.

"Sssh, Milly! Dad might hear. Oh my goodness, Annabelle, I can see the panelled wall. We just need to move the bench to get to the bottom panel."

"Get down then, Harry, or I can't move the bench!" Both children gasped in amazement as a beautiful old wooden panelled wall was revealed behind the bench.

"Let's try and push." They both pushed together. Suddenly the bottom panel gave way. A gap just big enough for an adult to crouch down and squeeze through was revealed. It was pitch black behind the panel.

"I can't see anything. It's too dark. Harry, go and get the head torches. Quickly, we don't want Dad to come and see what we're doing."

Milly put her head in the gap behind the panel and sniffed. Her tail wagged and before Annabelle could stop her she had disappeared inside.

"Harry, thank goodness you're back. Milly is inside and I can't see her." With that there was the faint sound of a dog barking, coming from the gap behind the wall. The children switched on their head torches.

"We've got to go in now and make sure Milly is okay," said Harry urgently. Bravely he crouched down and stepped into the darkness behind the fireplace. Annabelle dropped the tapestry back down and pulled the bench against the wall behind her. At least if Mum and Dad did come into the lounge they wouldn't guess where they'd gone. She wasn't sure she wanted to follow Harry into the darkness, but they had to get Milly.

"Look, Annabelle, it's the spiral staircase just like Elise described!" said Harry. His voice echoed around the walls as he stepped down around the bend in the staircase. Annabelle watched him quickly disappear out of sight and further underground. The steps were incredibly uneven. Annabelle stepped carefully and slowly. She didn't want to trip, unlike Harry who, it seemed, was going as fast as he could!

Suddenly she heard a familiar noise.

"Harry, is that Milly? Is she going 'cracker dog?'" That was what they called it when Milly went crazy if she hadn't seen you for a while. She would squeal with excitement and run round and round chasing her tail like a crazy dog! She must have been so happy to see Harry.

Annabelle turned the corner to see Milly sitting on Harry's knee and in front of them was a very old wooden door. Milly jumped up and went "cracker dog" all over again at seeing Annabelle. Harry was grinning from ear to ear and in his hand was the key they had found under the floorboards.

"What a relief, Harry! I'd totally forgotten we needed the key. Have you tried it to see if it unlocks the door?"

"I was just about to! I found Milly at the bottom of the stairs here scratching at the door."

Annabelle held her breath as Harry placed the key into the lock. He tried to turn it, but with no luck.

"Give it a wiggle," said Annabelle. Harry wiggled the key. It turned in the lock and the door opened with a loud creak. Annabelle shone her head torch through the door. The tunnel was cut into the rock.
It was dark and smelt damp.

"I think if we follow this tunnel we should get to the cavern bit by the beach that we were in the other day," said Annabelle. "I imagine the boulder will be across but we can just follow the tunnel back to the cottage once we've seen it."

"Sounds like a good plan. I'll go first!" said Harry.

Annabelle was relieved. She didn't really want to lead the way. Harry ran past her and into the tunnel. Milly was at his heel. Annabelle followed as fast as she could. It was cold in the tunnel and smelt musty. After a while Harry turned a corner. He had come out at a crossroads which intersected with the other tunnel.

"Annabelle, come quickly!"

Annabelle ran round the corner to meet him. She was out of breath.

"Look," said Harry, "if you stand here and face in the direction of the tunnel from the cottage it's set back and around this corner. It's just as Elise said. You would never spot the second tunnel if you came from the beach or the church. That's probably why it's remained secret for so long. This tunnel to the left must be the tunnel to the church. If we follow this one it should go to the beach!"

Harry was delighted with himself. He still couldn't believe that there was a smuggler's tunnel leading from their holiday cottage. It was amazing.

"Come on! Let's follow the tunnel to the beach," said Annabelle. Harry responded by running past her with Milly. As they got nearer to the beach they could see shafts of light entering the tunnel.

"Stop, Harry!" shouted Annabelle. For once Harry

stopped and ran back to her. They could see the cavern in front of them. Annabelle pulled Harry down into the shadows at the back.

"Look!" she whispered, pointing. "There's light coming in from the entrance. Someone's using the tunnel. They could be coming from the beach, or maybe from the church?"

Harry jumped as the sound of men's voices echoed around the cavern. They saw two dark figures at the entrance to the tunnel. They must have been on the beach. Maybe getting more jewels and coins from the wreck.

"Quick, we need to hide. Turn off your head torch!" Annabelle grabbed Harry's hand, and with the other felt along the wall of the tunnel, pulling Harry after her. She could feel Milly at her heels. She was hoping that just like Elise she would feel the opening in the rock. It was useless, though, it just wasn't there and the men were getting closer.

Then, just as the men had started to move towards the back of the cavern she found it. She pulled Harry into the gap and they crouched down in the darkness scared to breathe in case the men heard them.

Harry was terrified Milly might bark or growl. Luckily he had two fruit pastilles in his pocket which he was saving for later. He gave one to Milly, hoping it wasn't the blackcurrant one which was his favourite. He could hear her chewing away. Hopefully that would stop her barking. He squeezed Annabelle's hand in the darkness. She squeezed back. He could feel her shaking with fear.

"Come on, shift it. We need to get this lot up to the church and get it hidden," said one of the men. He sounded like he was in a hurry.

"Don't, *whatever you do*, drop any," said the other man. "If you lose any of the jewels again he will seriously lose it with you. He's waiting for us at the church, you know."

"I know. Anyway – high tide tomorrow and we should have all the stuff off the wreck. I can't wait to get it sold, give him his money and then he should leave us alone."

At that moment Milly finished chewing her sweet and started growling. Harry put his hand down to quieten her but instead, in the darkness he stroked the floor of the tunnel. It was then he felt something small and round. He picked it up and put it in his pocket. He must remember to look at whatever it was when they were back in the light. Luckily, Annabelle had taken care of Milly.

"What's that noise?" The men stopped right outside the opening where the children and Milly were hiding. It went quiet as the men listened. Harry shut his eyes and held his breath. Annabelle stroked Milly and held her close. She crossed her fingers that she wouldn't make a sound.

"Can't hear anything mate. No one knows about this tunnel. Why would there be anyone in here? It's probably a rat or something. Come on. He'll be really cross if we're late."

The children heard the men running up the tunnel in the direction of the church.

"I think we should follow them," whispered Harry, even though he felt afraid. "If we did we could find out where they're hiding the treasure and who 'he' is. What do you think?"

Annabelle swallowed. She didn't want to, but she knew it was the right thing to do.

"Let's do it for Elise," she said, quietly.

"Come on then. I think the men have gone. I'll go in front and hold my head torch in my hand then I can turn it off quickly if I need to."

Once again the tunnel ahead lit up. The children moved quietly along the tunnel after the men. Milly kept close. They knew that soon they would be at the church. What was waiting for them? The next piece of the jigsaw or being caught and the thieves realising the "DNA Detectives" were after them?

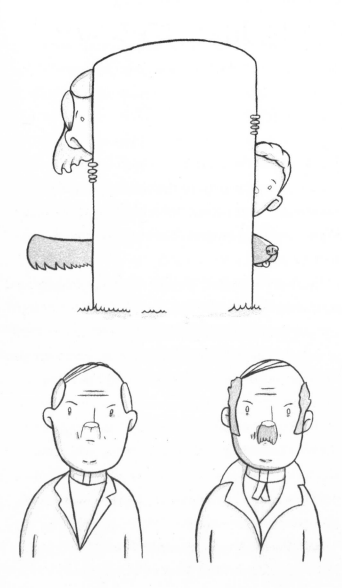

Chapter 12
Hidden treasure

(A)nnabelle and Harry listened at the wooden door which led to the bell tower in the church. Milly sat silently at their feet. It was as if she knew she had to be quiet. There was no sound. The men must have gone already.

Harry stuck his thumb up to Annabelle and pointed it towards the door. He hoped she'd got the message that he thought the coast was clear and he was going inside. He didn't dare speak in case the men were still there and heard them. Annabelle nodded. Harry put his hand against the door and slowly pushed it open. He beckoned to Annabelle and they tiptoed quietly into the bell tower. Once there, they slowly opened the second door and peered into the church.

"They aren't here, Harry. Let's have a look in the graveyard."

He followed Annabelle to the door of the church. Milly was close behind. They crept out and hid together behind a gravestone. Annabelle peered out.

"There they are, Harry. I can't see who it is, though. They're too far away. What are they doing?"

Milly growled.

"I don't know," said Harry. "It looks like they're crouched down. They must be burying the treasure! Hold on, the vicar is going over to them. He's going to catch them red-handed. Do you think we should call the police? He'll need some help."

It was so exciting – the men were going to be caught by the vicar. It would all be over soon!

"Hold on, Harry. Look… they're all shaking hands! The men are giving him something. It looks like a long black tool. Now he's on the floor. I think he must be involved. Oh no! The men are heading back to the beach. I can't believe the vicar is involved! Do you remember what Josh told us about the vicar? It looks like he's helping smugglers too, just like his great-great-grandfather all those years ago!"

"Maybe that's why he gives us such horrible looks when he see's us. He thinks we took the locket from him! Watch out, Annabelle. He's coming this way!"

Annabelle and Harry ran back into the church with Milly and pretended to look at the stained glass windows.

"I don't think he saw us, do you?"

At that moment the door to the church swung

open. The vicar came storming in at quite a pace. He stopped in his tracks when he saw the children, as if he was surprised to see them there.

As the vicar walked towards them Harry nudged Annabelle and whispered, "Look at the old tool he's carrying. It's an old spring well hook, just like the tool we saw in the museum. The tool used by smugglers to hide their goods in a well!"

"Maybe it belonged to his great-great-grandfather! They must be hiding the treasure in a well! It must be the well that Elise had seen Henry and his gang hiding their loot in all those years ago," said Annabelle.

The children stepped forward trying to get a better look at the tool. The vicar realised the children had seen it and tried to hide it behind his back. If there was any doubt of his involvement before, there was none now. He looked red and agitated.

"What're you two doing here?" asked the vicar in a gruff voice. Milly ran forward and barked at him. To their horror, he pushed her off aggressively. She whined and cowered at the children's feet.

"We were uummhh…" Harry didn't know what to say. The vicar looked really cross.

Just in time, Annabelle remembered Alice, the lady in the museum, telling them that Elise was buried here in the church. "We're looking for the grave of

Elise Andersdatter. The girl who was the only survivor from the ship wreck *The Helena*. The girl who was taken in by the family who owned the inn."

"It's the last grave by the wall that looks out to sea. Now get out of my church and take your scrawny dog with you," said the vicar. With that, he gave them one more angry look and hurried off to the bell tower, making sure he hid the tool out of sight.

"That's such a relief! I don't think he knows we saw them. Let's go and see if we can find Elise's grave," said Annabelle to Harry. The two of them walked in the direction the vicar had said. Milly seemed much happier. Her tail wagged as she trotted after Harry who was reading the inscriptions on the gravestones.

"Here it is!" said Harry, delighted he had found it before Annabelle.

"Look, there are fresh flowers on the grave," said Annabelle. "I think they must have been from the lady we saw the other day when we got trapped in the tunnel from the beach. I wonder if she knew Elise. Maybe they were related."

She crouched down to read the inscription on the headstone:

"Elise Andersdatter, March 8th 1871 – April 25th 1963. Daughter of Anders & Helena

Andersdatter, adopted by the Nance family of this parish. Only survivor of the wrecked ship The Helena our beloved daughter is once again returned to us.

We are tied to the ocean. And when we go back to the sea, whether it is to sail, or to watch, we are going back from whence we came."

"I think those words are beautiful," she said, "and look, the grave is looking out to sea. I think she's looking out at the ocean to where she last saw her parents." They looked down towards the beach. "I think she must've been happy in the end. Remember in her diary she said she really liked Henry's wife Jenny and their children Jago and Gwen. I wonder why, then, that I just get the feeling she's unhappy."

Annabelle shivered. The sky suddenly turned dark and a cold wind whipped around the graveyard.

"I think we should go. I don't like it here anymore," said Harry. "I think we should go to the other bit of the graveyard where the men and the vicar were. I think if we have a look there we might be able to find where the well is and the treasure."

"I agree, Harry. The atmosphere here feels troubled. I can't see the vicar. Let's go now."

She ran behind Harry to the part of the graveyard where they'd seen the men. Milly had found some apples on the floor. She brought one to Annabelle and dropped it on the ground for her to throw. If Milly didn't have a ball she often found something else for the children to throw for her. Today it was an apple!

"All I can see is this statue of an angel and a big apple tree," said Harry. By the sound of his voice Annabelle could tell he was losing interest already. Milly barked at Annabelle to get her to throw the apple.

"Come on, Harry. Remember Elise said the well was near a statue of an angel and it's on the floor. We need to search round here. Okay, Milly! I'll throw it for you!"

Annabelle picked up the apple and threw it as far as she could. She looked at Harry, who seemed to have regained his enthusiasm. Harry had realised that searching meant he got to kick the fallen leaves into the air. With great delight, he kicked some of the leaves over Annabelle.

"Stop it, Harry. That's not funny!" Seeing the leaves in Annabelle's hair and the cross expression on her face made Harry laugh uncontrollably. He fell on the floor. As he did, he hit something hard on the ground. He wiped the ground with his hand to reveal a wooden circular lid. He stopped laughing, realising he had found the well.

"Annabelle, I've found it!" shouted Harry.

Annabelle forgot about being cross with him. Quickly and with much excitement she helped Harry push back the rest of the leaves and turf that had been used to cover the lid of the well. She couldn't wait to look down it and find out if they could see the treasure.

"Oh no! There's a padlock on it," said Harry, sounding disappointed. "I could try and smash it with a stone?"

It was then they heard someone shout very loudly.

"Oi! You two! Get away from there!"

"Quick, it's the vicar! Help me cover up the well Harry. He mustn't know we have found it!"

"Come on, Annabelle. We need to get away! Run!" Annabelle followed Harry, running faster than she'd ever run before. Milly was close behind. Annabelle could hear the vicar shouting and he was shaking his fist in the air at them. They just had to make it onto the road where there were other people and then they would be safe. The gate seemed like forever away. The vicar was now giving chase and gaining on them.

Harry could feel his legs getting tired. Would they be able to escape before the vicar caught them? Did the vicar know they had found the well? Harry's heart pounded in his chest. They had to get away. They just had to!

Chapter 13
Revealing results

"I can see the holiday cottage," said Harry.
"Come on, Annabelle – we're nearly home."

Annabelle was so relieved. She looked behind her.
Luckily the vicar must've given up the chase. She
followed Harry up the drive but it looked like they
had jumped out of the frying pan into the fire.

"Look, Mum's back from the university. She's
waiting for us and she looks really cross." Harry could
see Mum waiting for them with her hands on her hips.
She was tapping her foot angrily.

"Where've you two been? Your dad and I couldn't
find you anywhere. We were worried."

"We just went to see Josh and Ellie. Sorry, Mum.
Is the barbeque ready?" said Harry. It did amaze
Annabelle how easily he could come up with a story.
It was a good one too.

"Well, next time tell Dad where you're going. He
was really worried. Come on, let's get some sausages.
You too, Milly!"

* * *

Annabelle couldn't bear the wait. They knew that soon the men would be making their last dive and it would be their only chance to catch them with the stolen goods, but they had to wait for the DNA results to come back from the university. Finally, in the afternoon, Mum had a phone call. When she finished she called Harry and Annabelle into the kitchen. She didn't sound happy.

"I've just had a call from the university. They found something odd about the samples. I don't suppose you two know anything about that, do you?"

Annabelle and Harry shook their heads. Annabelle tried her hardest not to look guilty.

Mum sounded cross. "Apparently eight of the samples are exactly the same and it looks like the person who gave one of the other samples was originally from Norway! Why would someone who has lived their whole life in Cornwall be originally from Norway? It doesn't make sense. Did you mess around with the samples you gave me from your friends? The result for the eight samples is odd. It means they must be from the same person."

"Really, it wasn't anything to do with us," said

Annabelle and Harry. They were delighted as they knew what that result meant – they had worked out who the thieves were.

"Why do you look so happy? I'm going to have to repeat the testing!" Mum started working on her iPad. Annabelle grabbed Harry and they ran upstairs to their bedroom.

"Am I right, Annabelle?" said Harry. "If eight of the samples were the same it means it must have been the twins, the surf instructors Alex and Peter. They did it! Because the DNA from identical twins would be the same. There were eight samples for the twins in total. One from each of the two sets of mouthpieces, diving masks and flippers we found in the tunnel – that makes six. Then one from Alex's flip-flop and one from Peter's sunglasses."

"You're right, Harry. The Norwegian sample must be Mum's mistake. Oh my goodness, who would've thought it was Alex and Peter, the surf instructors! They're so friendly. But we did see them talking to the vicar, who we know is also involved, and he was really cross with them. Maybe because they dropped the locket?"

"They're also young, have Cornish accents and work locally," added Harry.

"We've got fingerprints from the mirror for each

twin, the fingerprints from the book from the library and the diving masks from the diving gear. Come on Harry – let's compare them. Identical twins may have the same DNA but they'll have different fingerprints. If we can find a match we can prove along with the DNA that both Alex and Peter were involved."

Annabelle pulled out the evidence from under the bed. Harry grabbed a magnifying glass from the "DNA Detectives" kit. They spread the evidence in front of them. "Harry, you look to see if you can find fingerprints from Peter," said Annabelle, "and use the fingerprints from the mirror as a reference. I'll look for Alex's prints."

"Alex has a loop pattern," said Harry his face close to the prints. "Of course I have a tented arch which is very rare."

"So do I!" said Annabelle. "Peter has a loop pattern too. But look – the ridges in the skin occur in different places. So it makes them different." She loved spot-the-difference games.

"Oh yes. When you look at the ridges there are lots of differences. I've got a match for Peter on the book from the library and…" Harry did a fake drum roll on his lap, "yes, on the diving mask from the tunnel. He was definitely there!"

Annabelle was gutted she hadn't found Alex's fingerprints so quickly.

"Hold on. Look, just there at the bottom of the page. It's Alex's print and he's on the diving mask too. Harry, now we've got the evidence we need to prove the twins were involved. We know the treasure is in the well. We've got to tell the police so they can catch them red-handed. They'll be diving down for the last haul on the next high tide which…" she ran to the window to look, "…is very soon! We need to tell Mum and Dad and get them to call the police!"

✳ ✳ ✳

Annabelle and Harry told Mum and Dad everything. The conversation was then repeated to the local police who came immediately. The police planned to capture Alex, Peter and the vicar, but first they needed access to the smuggler's tunnel that ran from the holiday cottage. Annabelle and Harry were delighted to show the police and their police dogs the entrance to the tunnel. Milly didn't seem too pleased with other dogs on her territory, though. She was even more put out when Harry offered the other dogs some of her beefy bone treats.

"No thank you, son," said one of the police officers. "Not when the dogs are on duty. They've got a job to do! Now, can you show me where the tunnel is please?"

"Follow me," said Annabelle. She took them into the lounge, lifted up the tapestry on the wall and pushed back the bench to reveal the panelling. She pushed the panel at the bottom to reveal the tunnel entrance. Harry handed the police officer the key. Annabelle looked over at Mum and Dad who were watching open mouthed. Even the policemen seemed surprised. They disappeared into the tunnel led by the police dogs.

"Quick, let's see what's happening outside," said Harry, as the policemen disappeared into the tunnel. The children ran to the bottom of the garden where they could see the beach.

"Look up there!" said Harry pointing. Annabelle looked. She could see police officers spread out along the cliffs. They were crouched down out of sight and watching the beach.

"Look, that officer has binoculars. He must be looking at the entrance to the tunnel on the beach waiting for the men to go in. Good job we were able to show them where it was," said Harry.

"That's right, son," said the officer who had stayed in the cottage with them. "That's exactly what they're doing. Not long now. I've just had a message over the radio that the men from the surf club have been spotted near the entrance to the tunnel on the beach. Hold on. I'm receiving another message – it's all systems go! I repeat: all systems go!"

Next, the children saw the police officers on the cliff stand up and start running at full pelt down onto the beach.

"Harry, look," said Annabelle, "it's just like a scene out of Elise's diary, with the customs officers running down onto the beach to catch Henry Nance and his men."

"Although this time they can't escape as the police officers are waiting in the secret tunnel!" said Harry.

"I hope so. It could still go wrong."

Waiting was agony. Would the police catch Alex and Peter red-handed with the jewels? What about the vicar? Would he be caught too? *Please don't let him get away*, thought Annabelle.

Chapter 14
Who owns the treasure?

T here was a knock at the door of the holiday cottage. Milly ran to the door barking.

"It's the police!" shouted Harry.

Mum pushed past him and Milly and opened the door. Annabelle ran to the corridor to hear the news. She almost dared not to listen, just in case she was disappointed.

"Hello officer, can we help?" said Mum to the police officer standing in the doorway.

"Hello," said the police officer. "I am Detective Andrews. We are pleased to inform you that, thanks to the information you provided, two suspects have been caught and arrested. They were in the old smuggler's tunnel as you suggested and we were able to retrieve a large number of gold coins from each of the suspects."

"Hurray!" shouted Annabelle and Harry, jumping up and down and hugging each other. "You do mean the twins Alex and Peter when you say suspects, don't you?" The detective nodded his head and smiled.

Then Annabelle remembered about the vicar. "What about the vicar?" she asked. "Did you catch him too? And the rest of the jewels – did you find them in the well?"

"So many questions!" replied the detective. "Well, the vicar seemed to realise that something had gone wrong when Alex and Peter didn't turn up. He decided to make a run for it, but not before taking the rest of the treasure out of the well. Caught him red-handed, we did, and with the tool the old smugglers used to get things out of the well! Now, this evidence you were talking about: the DNA and the fingerprints. We're going to need to see them. Can you show me?"

"I'm so sorry," said Mum. "They know you shouldn't take DNA without someone's permission. You've let me down, you two."

Annabelle and Harry looked to the floor.

"We're sorry, Mum," said Annabelle. "It was the only way to prove who the thieves were and get the treasure back." They explained to Mum about the samples from the university too.

"Can you take the police officer upstairs, please, to get your evidence? I'll print out a copy of the DNA results from the university for them."

"Thank you very much," said the police officer.

"Although don't be too harsh on them. I think without your children we may not have caught the thieves and the treasure would have been lost forever. Historic England, the charity, who own the wreck, are delighted the jewels and coins have been found. They..." the policeman tried to continue but was interrupted by Harry.

"But they don't belong to Historic England, they belong to the family of Elise Andersdatter, the only survivor of *The Helena*. They belonged to her mother."

"I was just going to say young man they're trying to find anyone that is directly related to Elise – I didn't know that was her name! So the jewels can be returned to the family. If they can't trace anyone they'll either go to the museum or be sold to raise some money for Historic England. I think the library are trying to trace the family in Norway."

As Annabelle heard what the police officer said, she was struck with a light bulb moment. Excitedly she called out, "I know how we can find them! Mum, didn't you say one of your samples came from someone from Norway? We didn't substitute all of the samples. Maybe that person might be related to Elise. Her family were from Norway. Do you remember when we got the 'smugglers' book from the library, one of the men told us that an old woman was looking for it? She had just moved back to the area and was researching her family tree. Maybe she was related to Elise. Can you see if there's a name for the Norwegian sample?"

Harry chipped in. "Don't you remember the lady from the graveyard, Annabelle? Do you remember she put flowers on Elise's grave? Maybe she knew her or is related to her. I wonder if she wrote in the visitor's book in the church."

"Goodness, what great detectives you are," said the police officer. "Let me know how you get on. I must get this evidence back to the station but I'll let you know if there are any developments."

With that he waved and was off to his car.

❉ ❉ ❉

"Mum's still cross with us, isn't she?" said Annabelle, feeling sad. She hated being in the wrong.

"She can't be that cross. She's looking to see if she has a name and address for the Norwegian sample," said Harry.

He's always positive, thought Annabelle. I'm going to try and be more like that.

Mum came running into the lounge to join them.

She was still holding her iPad and looked really excited, which made Annabelle smile.

"I've got some exciting news – a name! The Norwegian sample came from an old lady who is eighty years old. She's called Emily Harris. I know her surname isn't Andersdatter like Elise, but she probably got married which would mean her surname would change. They could still be related. I can't access the address on the computer at the moment but why don't we see if she wrote it in the visitor's book at the church. It should be easy to find her now we have a name. I'll grab Milly and then let's go."

"Mum, when we get back, will you explain how the scientists can work out where someone comes from by looking at their DNA?" asked Annabelle.

"Of course, Annabelle. But we need to go now or I think your brother will burst with excitement!"

Annabelle could wait till later but only just! She was fascinated at how your DNA was like a postcode to work out where in the world you originated from. It was incredible. She couldn't wait for Mum's explanation.

✳ ✳ ✳

The sun shone as they ran towards the church. Harry pushed open the door and then ran over to the table where the visitor's book had been the other day when they'd knocked it over. There it was, in the same place. Harry read the page that was open. He used his finger to scan for the name Emily. "Nothing!" he said, disappointed.

Annabelle stepped forward and turned the page. She browsed the list of names and there it was. "Got it! Look – 'Emily Harris, Pentreath House, Tresorporth.'"

"'Pentreath' means 'top of the beach' in Cornish," said Mum. "That's a good place to start looking! If not we can ask where it is in the shop. I'm sure they'll know. You know, if we do find this lady, the police have asked me to use DNA to prove she is related to your smuggler's adopted daughter Elise. I was thinking about the hair in the locket you found. You said that it's Elise's hair, right? We could try and get DNA from that and compare it with that of this lady. The DNA will tell us if they're related."

"How can you use the DNA to see if they're related?" asked Harry. He was genuinely interested.

"Do you remember in my workshop I explained
that DNA is protected in a special bag called a cell?"

"I told him that too," said Annabelle.

"Well there are two different sources of DNA
in your cells. The first is the DNA you get from
your mum and dad. You get half your DNA from
your mum and half from your dad and this is
called 'nuclear DNA'. This is because it's found in
something called the 'nucleus' which looks like a
round ball in the middle of the cell. This is the DNA
that makes you unique because you get a mixture
of DNA from your mum and your dad. The second
type of DNA is completely separate from 'nuclear
DNA' – it is called 'mitochondrial DNA'. This type
of DNA you get only from your mum. It's not found
in the nucleus like nuclear DNA. It's found in the
mitochondria which look a bit like jellybeans.

The mitochondria are the powerhouses of the cell; they are like a battery and help produce energy for our bodies to function. A brilliant thing about mitochondrial DNA is that the pattern of it stays the same from generation to generation. So, you and Harry – boys and girls! – will have the same pattern of mitochondrial DNA as me, and we have the same pattern of mitochondrial DNA as Grandma, we all have the same pattern as Grandma's Mum, and so on and so on. So if you have the same pattern of mitochondrial DNA as someone else you must be related. So if this lady is related to Elise they will have the same pattern of mitochondrial DNA. Do you remember the story about King Richard III whose skeleton was found in the car park in Leicester? Well, they used his family tree to locate his modern-day relatives. When they looked at the pattern of their mitochondrial DNA it was the same. This proved they were related and that the skeleton really was King Richard III. Isn't that amazing?"

"Ooh!" said Harry. "That's so exciting. We must find this lady and get her DNA!"

"Well, we need to ask her permission Harry. As you know you can't just take DNA without asking! Now – to the beach. We need to find Pentreath House."

*** *** ***

"Mum! What about that pink cottage? It's right at the top of the beach. I think I can see someone in the garden. And she's got grey hair!"

They all ran as fast as they could towards the pink cottage, including Milly, who sensed their urgency and wondered if there may be cake at their destination. The gate creaked as they entered and walked up the beautiful garden towards the old lady. They were met with the smell of roses and freshly cut grass. It was a very tranquil garden. A breeze blew gently in from the sea and there was the sound of seagulls above them.

"Hello my lovelies," said the old woman, getting up. She must be a local, they all thought. "My name's Emily. How can I help?"

Annabelle and Harry high fived one another. They were so delighted. They had found her. Then, as the woman got nearer, Annabelle noticed her feet. She was wearing open-toe sandals and Annabelle could see that she had six toes, just like Elise!

"Aaah! You spotted my funny foot. Got that from my mum and she got it from her mum. We all have funny feet in our family. How can I help you?"

Annabelle and Harry listened as their mother explained the situation to the lady.

"Well, how amazing," said Emily "I've only just moved back to find out more about my family history. Of course, Elise was my great-grandmother. She died when I was 26 years old. We moved away from Tresorporth several years ago but Elise used to tell me the most amazing stories of when she lived with a smuggler. They ran the Inn in Tresorporth for many years. Of course the Inn is now a holiday cottage."

"That's where we're staying!" said Harry, delighted. "We've been reading Elise's diary. The lady at the museum gave it to us."

"Well I never! You know I looked for that diary everywhere when the Inn was sold. Elise told me about it, you see, but then she got a bit forgetful as she got older and couldn't remember where she had hidden it!"

"It was behind the fireplace in the bedroom. The builders found the diary when they were taking the fireplace out. Did you know about the secret tunnel?"

"Of course! That's where we used to play as children when we would visit. But we were sworn to secrecy! Did you find the key under the floorboard?" The old lady smiled as she spoke. Annabelle guessed she had lots of happy memories of playing in that tunnel.

"It's still there!" said Harry, delighted.

"Well I never. That tunnel hasn't been used for years. Full of history, that tunnel. So you just need to take some DNA from me. Then if your mum can get DNA from the hair in the locket which is Elise's, she can prove that we're related. Is that right? I remember Elise talking about the locket and her mum's other jewellery. It meant so much to her. She was so upset that it was lost when *The Helena* sank. I would love to return it to our family."

Annabelle and Harry watched as Emily signed the consent form to say she was happy for them to test her DNA. Mum then used a cotton bud to wipe the inside of Emily's cheek. "She's collecting cells from Emily's cheek and they'll be full of DNA and mitochondrial DNA," said Harry, proudly.

"Thank you so much, Emily. Fingers crossed we can get DNA from the hair in the locket. I'm worried that the locket has been under the sea for about 130 years. If any sea water has got in, the chances of getting any DNA we can use will be small. However when you open the locket and look inside the lock of hair is sealed behind a small glass plate. I couldn't see any water inside which means it must be intact and airtight. So, fingers crossed, the DNA won't have been destroyed. We'll let you know the results as soon as we can. So lovely to meet you."

"You too," said Emily and waved goodbye to them all.

"Mum, is there really only a small chance you'll be able to get DNA from the locket?" said Annabelle, worried about what would happen to the jewels and coins if the DNA didn't work.

"Well, Emily has said she doesn't mind if we have to break the locket to get to the hair. The scientists at the university will carefully lift up the glass plate and hopefully get to the hair underneath. They'll then use chemicals to break open the cells and get the DNA out. You're right – it's only a small chance. But the scientists in the laboratory are used to getting DNA out of very old samples so there's still a good possibility! Don't give up yet. They're brilliant at what they do. I'll take the locket and the sample from Emily over to the university when I get back. We should get the results in a few days."

Annabelle crossed her fingers and nudged Harry to do the same. *Please let the DNA work,* thought Annabelle. If she wished really hard it might just happen.

Chapter 15
The Final Piece of the Jigsaw

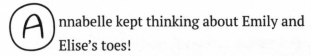

(A)nnabelle kept thinking about Emily and Elise's toes!

"Mum, do you remember Emily said her family had 'funny feet', and that she had got it from her Mum? Well we know from Elise's diary that she had six toes just like Emily. Would this have been passed down the family in their DNA?"

"They looked strange," said Harry, making a face.

"Sssh, Harry. That's right, Annabelle, it would. Do you remember what we call that process?"

Annabelle thought back to Mum's DNA workshop. Harry did too, but couldn't remember. He wished he could so he could out-trump Annabelle. Then with delight Annabelle remembered the word and proudly said, "Inheritance!"

"Fantastic, well done. As you know, inheritance is when your parents pass on their characteristics, features or even a disease through their DNA. Emily has 'inherited' her funny feet from her mother."

"I know the scientists at the university are already checking if Emily and Elise have the same pattern of mitochondrial DNA. If the pattern is the same it will prove they are related..." Annabelle hadn't quite finished when Harry interrupted:

"I know mitochondrial DNA is the one that you only get from your mum and is the same pattern over many generations if you are related. Mitochondria give us our energy and are the powerhouses in the cell!" He looked at Annabelle in a "you see I know stuff too" kind of way!

"Well done, Harry!" Mum looked impressed at what he had learnt.

"As I was saying, could we use the fact that Emily and Elise have 'funny feet' as another way to prove they were related?"

"Yes, we could. The more proof we can get that they are related the better. Well, what a coincidence. I was planning to take you to the Molecular Genetics Laboratory in Exeter tomorrow to meet my friends. That's the lab where I used to work. It was the best job I ever had! The laboratory is part of the hospital and they use DNA to study diseases that have been inherited by families. They help to identify what disease someone has or may develop later in life so the doctors can help to treat it, or even prevent it, if they can. I am sure they're working on polydactyl which is the name for someone who is born with extra toes or fingers. I'll give my old boss Jo a ring and see if she can help."

Annabelle and Harry whooped with excitement at the news. This might help Emily to get back the jewels that were rightfully hers! Mum went off to make the phone call. They waited with nervous anticipation.

"Exciting news, you two! I just heard from the university and spoke to my old boss. The university have been able to get DNA from Emily and the locket. They're just doing the analysis of the mitochondrial DNA now so we should find out the results tomorrow. They also agreed to send some of the DNA over to the Molecular Genetics Laboratory at the hospital in Exeter, so Jo and her team can test the samples and see if Emily and Elise's polydactyl was caused by the same mistake in their DNA. Jo has invited us over to the lab tomorrow so we can find out the results."

"But we can't wait! We need to know now!" said Harry, jumping up and down.

"It takes time, Harry. They're rushing the samples through for us as fast as they can. But you have to be patient. Sometimes the samples don't work either. Don't forget the DNA from the locket is very old. So don't get your hopes up too much."

Harry's face crumpled with disappointment. He looked across at Annabelle and could see she felt the same. He had thought now they had the DNA it would definitely work and they would get the result they wanted. Maybe it wasn't to be. Just one sleep and they would find out.

✳ ✳ ✳

It was a nervous drive to the hospital in Exeter. Mum had picked up Emily on the way. They all felt it was important for her to be there. Dad had stayed behind to look after Milly.

"We're here!" announced Harry. "Look at the sign 'Molecular Genetics Department'. He actually thought he might burst. He was fizzing with excitement, but had prepared for the awful possibility that they may have failed. Annabelle gave him a smile.

"Follow me," said Mum. Harry rushed ahead to hold open the door and they all followed Mum through the double doors of the huge building in front of them. They signed in and were given badges.

"All the laboratories for the hospital are here but on different floors," said Mum. "There's microbiology, immunology, pathology, and haematology – that's blood." Harry wasn't sure what all those departments did but he followed Mum into the Molecular Genetics Department. Annabelle smiled at Emily who looked a little nervous.

Mum knocked on a blue door which read "Professor Jo Carter. Head of Molecular Genetics Department."

"Come in," said a friendly voice.

The door opened and inside was a smartly dressed lady sitting behind a desk and an older man who was wearing glasses. The lady spoke again.

"Hello, I'm Jo," she said to the children and Emily. "Mandy, how are you? Great to see you. Don't forget to say hello to everyone in the lab. They can't wait to catch up with you and meet your children! We've missed you."

That must be Mum's old boss thought Annabelle, as Jo gave Mum a hug. It was funny hearing Mum being called by her first name.

Jo continued. "This is Nick. He's come over from the university to talk about the results. Would anyone like a drink? I've got tea, coffee or water. I'm sure you can't wait to hear what we have found out!"

Annabelle and Harry nodded their heads in great excitement. Mum pulled out a chair for Emily to sit on. Annabelle thought Emily looked really nervous.

Annabelle looked around the small room. Jo was busy making cups of tea from a kettle in the corner.

Behind her were timetables and a huge picture of a beautiful DNA double helix on the wall. In the corner were several grey filing cabinets, with contents all neatly labelled. Annabelle looked at Jo's desk where there were three trays one on top of the other full of reports and papers. She spotted several yellow post-it notes stuck to the phone but she couldn't see what they said. On the other wall was a bookshelf full of journals and books about cell biology and genetics. Harry had spotted the photo on Jo's desk.

"Is that your daughter?" he asked Jo.

"It is!" said Jo, looking amused.

Mum smiled at them all and said, "These are my children, Annabelle and Harry. As you can see they're very excited! This is Emily. We're really hoping you can prove that she's related to Elise – the smuggler's adopted daughter."

"Well, I think we should get cracking," said Jo. "You all look very nervous. First of all I need to explain some terms to you. If you were making a Lego model. Let's say for example a model of a helicopter." Harry nodded his approval at her choice of model, and she went on. "You would need to use the instructions in the box to tell you how to build it. Well, human DNA is just like that. It's the instructions to make a human, the instructions to make you! All the information you need to make the Lego Helicopter are found in one instruction booklet. Guess how many instruction booklets you need to make a human?"

"Is it 30?" said Annabelle.

"46!" said Jo "But we don't call them instruction booklets, we call them 'chromosomes' and they're made of DNA. Emily has a mistake in the DNA in one of her instruction booklets – 'chromosomes' – which has caused her to have extra toe." Emily smiled.

Jo went on. "If you look in the instruction booklet to make a Lego model you'll find they are separated into pages and on each page are the instructions to make a different part of the model. Like the propellers or the cabin for the pilot. Our chromosomes are like this, split into pages to make different parts of us. But instead of 'pages' we call them 'genes'. In fact humans have about 20,000 genes in total split between the 46 instruction booklets (or chromosomes). Emily, the mistake in your DNA is in your instruction booklet number 7, your Chromosome 7. The page of the instruction booklet where the mistake is 'the gene' is called GLI3! This gene helps control how your fingers and toes develop when you're in your mum's tummy before you're born. If there is a mistake in it then you will be born with an extra toe or finger. How many letters are there in the alphabet?"

"26!" said Annabelle. She knew she was right.

"Correct! Well DNA has only four letters, **G**uanine, **C**ytosine, **T**hymine and **A**denine. We call them **G**, **T**, **A** and **C** for short. Your DNA is made up of a pattern of 3 billion Gs, Ts, As and Cs, and scientists can determine what this pattern is using special machines. We compared Emily and Elise's DNA with the pattern of DNA from someone who doesn't have polydactyl. We found that you both have a rare mistake. You have what we call a 'deletion'. So you're missing an A and a G compared to other people. Polydactyl, having an extra finger or toe, is quite common. One in five hundred people will be born with an extra finger or toe. But your mistake, or what we call a 'mutation', is very rare. In fact when we looked at the database no one else has been found with the same mistake in their DNA. Therefore we can say there's a really good chance that you, Emily, are related to Elise because you have the same mutation in your DNA which has caused your extra toe."

"Well I never!" said Emily.

"I've more news," said Nick, sitting forward. "We couldn't get DNA from the hair in the locket because it had been cut rather than pulled out of someone's head. This meant there were no roots on the hair so there were no cells. As you know, the cells are where the DNA is so there was no DNA in the hair."

For a moment, Annabelle and Harry's hearts plummeted. They looked at each other both feeling utterly disappointed.

"But there was something funny that happened," Nick went on, "It turned out Elise had lots of dandruff! We found lots inside the locket. Dandruff is formed from the skin on your scalp which flakes off. It's full of cells and therefore, of course, full of DNA! We're lucky that the seal on the locket was not broken, so sea water had not got into it which would've destroyed the DNA. Even though the sample is over 130 years old we were able to get lots of DNA!"

"Yes!" shouted Annabelle and Harry in relief.

"I remember Elise always used to complain about her dandruff!" said Emily. "Little did she know that one day her dandruff would be used to help her family. I wonder if Elise had realised, she might not have complained so much!"

"We were able to look at mitochondrial DNA from Emily and Elise," said Jo, "and determine where they originally came from and even more importantly that their pattern of DNA was exactly the same, which means they are definitely related!"

"Can you explain how you can use DNA to find out where someone comes from?" said Annabelle. "Mum was supposed to but she forgot!"

"Go on Mandy, you explain to the children," said Jo, and she and Nick laughed.

Mum rummaged in her bag and brought out a packet of jelly babies and some cocktail sticks. "Lucky I had these. We're having a party later," explained Mum.

"Okay, we need to sort the jelly babies into four colours to represent the Gs, Ts, As and Cs that make up the DNA. Now bite off their bodies and give me their heads." Annabelle and Harry took great delight in doing this and handed her back the different coloured heads.

"In 2003 the Wellcome Trust Sanger Institute, which is a huge laboratory in Cambridge, helped to complete the Human Genome Project and determine the entire pattern of DNA – the pattern of Gs, Ts, As and Cs – for one person. This pattern I'm making now out of jelly babies represents a very small part of this person's DNA."

They all watched as Mum threaded six of the jelly baby heads onto the cocktail stick.

"I'm using yellow for G, blackcurrant for T, orange for A and green for C," said Mum. Harry's tummy rumbled! "The scientists then looked at the pattern of Gs, Ts, As and Cs from the next person. When they compared

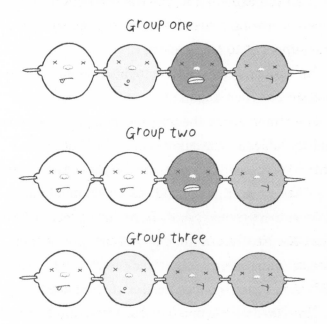

Group one

Group two

Group three

them with the pattern from the first person they found it was different. They decided to call the pattern from the first person 'Group 1' and decided to call the pattern from the second person 'Group 2'.

Mum threaded exactly the same colour jelly baby heads onto the second cocktail stick but changed one so it was green rather than yellow.

"When they looked at the next person they found it was different again and the pattern from the third person became 'Group 3'. The more people they looked at, the pattern of their DNA seemed to fall into either Group 1, Group 2 or Group 3. Then they found someone with a different pattern again. They called this 'Group 4', and so on and so on. Scientists love to find patterns and sort things out. The more people they looked at, the more they fell into these different groups. But something interesting happened when they looked at where these people came from. They saw that all the people from Group 1 came from Europe, Group 2 came from South Asia, Group 3 came from Native America and Group 4 came from Africa, and so on. So they realised that, by looking at your DNA, we can find out where in the world you originated from."

"That's amazing, Mum. Can I eat these now?" said Harry although he did remember to share with Annabelle.

"Thanks for explaining that," said Nick, smiling at Mum. "When we looked at DNA from Elise and Emily we found they both came from the west of Norway and Cornwall."

"Elise's father came from Bergen and her mother was Cornish," said Emily. "As was my mother. We've always lived in Cornwall. I'm amazed that the Norwegian DNA is still there in my DNA. Like an atlas to the past! It makes total sense. Thank you for finding the answers and proving we're related. Of course I know that we're related but this is the proof we needed and I'm grateful."

Annabelle and Harry hugged Emily. As Harry leant over something fell out of his pocket. They watched it as it rolled across the floor, spun and fell at Emily's feet. She picked it up.

"Where did you get this?" she said.

"I'd totally forgotten I picked it up from the floor when I was hiding in the smuggler's tunnel. Do you think it's Elise's lucky penny?"

"I do, my love. I do. It always made her so sad that she lost it. It was so special to her. She was sure she'd dropped it in the tunnel and asked us to look for it but no one ever found it."

She clasped it in her hand and let out a big sigh.

"This would make her so happy. We need to give it back you know," she said winking at the children.

✳ ✳ ✳

As Emily, the Wallace family and Milly walked towards Elise's grave at the church overlooking the beach, Mum said, "I heard from the police. They found DNA on the tool the thieves used to hide the goods in the well, the lid of the well and the jewels. The DNA matched all three men. They also found fingerprints on the tool from the well which matched the book from the library. A search of computers found in the men's homes and their phones revealed that the men planned to sell the jewels for a lot of money. The DNA, fingerprints, computer and phone evidence and the fact that they were caught red-handed meant the police had a very strong case! They've been charged with stealing treasure from the wreck, not claiming their finds and intending to sell the treasure. The police think they'll be off to prison for a long time and it's all thanks to you! The police are very grateful for your help."

Mum and Dad hugged Annabelle and Harry, and Milly tried to join in.

"I've decided to donate the jewellery and the locket to the museum," said Emily. "It's such a great story. I want it to be told. But I think now we've something important to do."

Harry smiled. Annabelle helped him dig a little hole in the ground in front of Elise's headstone. They placed the lucky penny carefully into it and then covered it over.

Emily placed some roses in a pot to cover the exposed soil. "They were her favourites," she said smiling.

As she finished the sun came out from behind a cloud. As the sun sparkled on the waves they all looked out from the grave to the sea and the spot where *The Helena* sunk and where this story had first started.

"I feel the atmosphere has changed," said Annabelle. "It feels happier. I think Elise is at peace."

Emily smiled and Annabelle noticed a tear running down her cheek. The story was complete and it was all due to the "DNA Detectives". It had been so much fun she wished that maybe in the future there would be another adventure. Although maybe not quite yet!

Acknowledgements

There are so many people who have helped me
with this book that I would like to thank, but first
and foremost I would like to thank my children,
Annabelle and Harry, and our dog Milly, who were
the inspiration for the characters in this book.
I know exactly how they would all behave in every
situation as I know them so well and they are such
different characters. Being able to write in the book
about funny situations that have happened to us
in real life has enabled me to keep our beautiful
memories as a family alive forever.

I would also like to thank my husband,
Jonathan, who has given me great encouragement
and been incredibly supportive throughout. He
also held the fort while I was away in Cornwall for
my very special research trip. I will always be very
grateful for your help.

A big thank you to my mum for accompanying
me on our trip to Cornwall, watching me eat
endless cream teas and your patience in listening

and encouraging me while I got excited about all my endless ideas for the story. A big thank you to Mum and Dad for taking us to Cornwall as children, which very much formed the inspiration for this book. Thank you also to Debbie, Ant, Alice, Emily, Alan, Virginia, Chris, Jo, Evie, Issy, Joanna, Nick, Alex and Peter for reading the book and giving me your valuable feedback. I am very grateful for all your enthusiasm and the encouragement you have given me. What a great family!

I would also like to thank Ben Duffy and his team at SJH Publishing for helping put together this book. It looks amazing. To Ben and my book agent Chloe Seager at Diane Banks Associates thank you for believing in me and making my dream become a reality.

A very special thank you to Jamie Maxwell for providing the fantastic illustrations for this book. After a short discussion he came up with the front cover and the images inside the book and knew exactly what was needed. Jamie, they are perfect. Thank you for making my stories come alive.

A huge thank you to the public engagement team at the Sanger Institute in Cambridge – Ken, Steve, Fran, Emily and Becky – for your encouragement, advice, support and helping with the web links for this book.

Thank you to all the staff at Jamaica Inn for looking after my mum and me so well and letting us look around the museum. I really got a flavour of the tools of the trade used by ship wreckers and smugglers. It gave me so many ideas and I think added so much authenticity to the story. I am very grateful for your contribution.

I would also like to thank Simon, Juliet, Henry and Oscar, my friends who live in Mullion Cove, and Jacqui Valender, who runs the guest house where we stayed on our trip to Cornwall. You all looked after us so well on our trip and gave me some great books about smugglers and advice on where the best smugglers' coves were. I will always be very grateful, and Jacqui I still have my lucky stone!

The laboratory I talk about in this book is based on the Genetics Department at the Royal Devon and Exeter NHS Foundation Trust where I was Deputy Manager testing for hereditary diseases. It was one of my favourite places to have worked, and with the best team. The head of the laboratory in the book is based on my good friend and manager of this department, Professor Sian Ellard. I want to say thank you so much to Sian and all my friends who work there for their support and encouragement with the book – I wanted to get you into the story and what better way! Thank you for looking after me so well when I was in Devon and for all the cream teas!

Finally, thank you to my friends, all the families who attend my DNA workshops/stories and to the children at the many schools, libraries and home-schooling groups who I have met through my work. Your excitement and encouragement when I have told you about my books has meant so much to me. So many of you have told me how much you loved the first book (which is wonderful to hear) and have asked "when is the next book coming out? We need to have it!" Well, wait no longer, it is finally here and you get to read it! Thank you for all your support. It is magical sharing my love of science and reading with you all.

Real world DNA detectives

The Wellcome Genome campus in Cambridge is home to the Wellcome Sanger Institute, one of the world's largest DNA research centres. But what is DNA and why is it so important to understand and study it?

As you will find out in this book, DNA is an amazing molecule that contains the biological instructions to make all living things, including us! Everyone's DNA is slightly different – this is what makes us unique. That is why we can use it to solve crimes and explore family history.

However, DNA is not just used to solve crimes, it can help us to understand how our bodies work.

At the Sanger Institute, scientists use special machines called DNA sequencers to read the code of DNA. All of the DNA instructions to make up a human – or any other living thing for that matter – are called a genome.

The machines we use are changing all the time. They are getting faster at reading DNA but also a lot cheaper so we can do more! Did you know, the first human genome was sequenced in 2000? It took over ten years and cost billions of dollars! Today we can sequence a whole human genome in a few hours – all for the cost of a new smart-phone.

Studying genomes can help scientists understand how the body works and what makes people ill. This helps them to find new ways of testing for illnesses and also make new medicines to help people get better.

Have you ever had the flu? Well, flu is caused by a virus and scientists can use DNA to work out and track where that flu virus came from, how it spread and whether it is changing. That's real medical detective work!

Did you know you can also use DNA to find out about people from the past? Scientists have used DNA taken from skeletons to find out more about where they come from and who they were. A great example is the story of King Richard III. His skeleton was hidden for centuries but was found in a car park in Leicester on 2013. DNA tests gave scientists the proof they needed to say it was the lost king. The DNA also told them that he had blond hair and blue eyes – that was a surprise because most paintings showed him with black hair!

But this science is not just for ancient skeletons. Did you know there are tests that can tell you about your ancestors – could you be related to a Viking or even a past king or queen?

When you think about it, more and more people are having some sort of experience with DNA technology: new vaccines, new medicines, DNA tests you can buy online. As you read this book, scientists are working away on the next big DNA breakthrough that could help you.

If you are a budding DNA Detective like Annabelle and Harry and want to find out more about the amazing molecule of life and the ways DNA is used to solve cutting-edge science challenges, visit our website **www.yourgenome.org**.

About the author

Mandy Hartley lives in Norfolk with her husband, two children Annabelle (aged 11) and Harry (aged 8), and Milly a black cockapoo. She has a PhD in Genetics and worked for 15 years in various different laboratories using DNA to study subjects as diverse as populations of fish at the genetic level, detecting inherited human diseases, criminal work and paternity and relationship testing. She now runs scientific workshops and performs stories to children. The stories she performs are designed to be multi-sensory and to help children with their understanding and visualisation of different scientific concepts.

Mandy wanted to create a series of science-based adventure books that were also educational, linking with many aspects of the curriculum for science and literacy. She has designed these stories so that the reader can see how the characters in the book use DNA to solve a mystery – just like real forensic scientists! At the same time, the reader

will learn all about DNA as part of the story.
Mandy wants to share her love and passion
for science with children and hopefully inspire
some future scientists.

This book has been granted a "green tick" by the Association for Science Education (ASE). It was reviewed by their education experts, who evaluated it to determine whether it was suitable for use in schools, and met all of the ASE criteria for quality. To read the full review and find out how ASE felt it could be used to help in the teaching of science and literacy at KS1 and KS2, go to **www.ase.org.uk/bookshop/reviews/the-dna-detectives/**